Dear Reader,

I am honored to once again participate in a Texas Cattleman's Club continuity.

No two people needed each other more than Zeke Travers and Sheila Hopkins, and getting the couple to realize that fact was both a challenge and a joy. Zeke and Sheila's story is a special one, and I hope you enjoy reading it as much as I enjoyed writing it. And I'm always excited when I can reunite my readers with characters from past books, such as Darius and Summer from my last Texas Cattleman's Club continuity book, *One Night with the Wealthy Rancher.*

I want to thank the other five authors who are a part of this continuity. I enjoyed working with each of you.

Happy reading!

Brenda Jackson

BRENDA JACKSON

TEMPTATION

Special thanks and acknowledgment to
Brenda Jackson for her contribution to the
Texas Cattleman's Club: The Showdown miniseries.

ISBN-13: 978-0-373-73133-6

TEMPTATION

Recycling programs
for this product may
not exist in your area.

Copyright © 2011 by Harlequin Books S.A.

www.Harlequin.com

Printed in U.S.A.

BRENDA JACKSON

is a die "heart" romantic who married her childhood sweetheart and still proudly wears the "going steady" ring he gave her when she was fifteen. Because she's always believed in the power of love, Brenda's stories always have happy endings. In her real-life love story, Brenda and her husband of thirty-eight years live in Jacksonville, Florida, and have two sons.

A *New York Times* bestselling author of more than seventy-five romance titles, Brenda is a recent retiree who now divides her time between family, writing and traveling with Gerald. You may write Brenda at P.O. Box 28267, Jacksonville, Florida 32226, by email at WriterBJackson@aol.com or visit her website, www.brendajackson.net.

To the love of my life, Gerald Jackson, Sr.

To the cast and crew of *Truly Everlasting—the Movie,*
this one is especially for you!
Thanks for all your hard work!

Though your beginning was small,
yet your latter end would increase abundantly.
—*Job* 8:7

* * *

Don't miss a single book in this series!

Texas Cattleman's Club: The Showdown
*They are rich and powerful, hot and wild.
For these Texans, it's showdown time!*

One

Some days it didn't pay to get out of bed.

Unless you had a tall, dark, handsome and naked man waiting in your kitchen to pour you a hot cup of coffee before sitting you in his lap to feed you breakfast. Sheila Hopkins smiled at such a delicious fantasy before squinting against the November sun that was almost blinding her through the windshield of her car.

And the sad thing was that she had awakened in a good mood. But all it had taken to spoil her day was a call from her sister that morning telling her she wasn't welcome to visit her and her family in Atlanta after all.

That message had hurt, but Sheila really should not have been surprised. What had she expected from her older sister from her father's first marriage? The same sister who'd always wished she hadn't existed? Definitely not any show of sisterly love at this late stage. If she hadn't shown any in Sheila's twenty-seven years, why had she assumed her sister would begin showing any now? Not her sister who had the perfect life with a husband who owned his own television station in Atlanta and who had two beautiful children and was pregnant with her third.

And if that very brief and disappointing conversation with Lois wasn't bad enough, she had immediately gotten a call from the hospital asking that she come in on her off day because they were shorthanded. And of course, being the dedicated nurse that she was, she had agreed to do so. Forget the fact she had planned to spend the day working in her garden. She didn't have a life, so did it really matter?

Sheila drew in a deep breath when she brought her car to a stop at a traffic light. She couldn't help glancing over at the man in the sports car next to her. She couldn't tell how the rest of him looked because she could only see his profile from the shoulders up, but even that looked good. And as if he'd known she was checking him out, he glanced her way. Her breath caught in her throat and her flesh felt tingly all over. He had such striking features.

They were so striking she had to blink to make sure they were real. Um…a maple-brown complexion, close-cut black hair, dark brown eyes and a chiseled jaw. And as she continued to stare at him, her mind mechanically put his face on the naked body of the tall, handsome man whom she would have loved to have found in her kitchen this morning. She inwardly chuckled. Neither she nor her kitchen would have been able to handle all the heat her imaginary lover would generate.

She saw his head move and realized he had nodded over at her. Instinctively, she nodded back. When his lips curved into a sensual smile, she quickly forced her gaze ahead. And when the traffic light changed, she pressed down on the gas, deciding to speed up a little. The last thing she wanted was to give the guy the impression she was flirting with him, no matter how good he looked. She had learned quickly that not all nicely wrapped gifts contained something that was good for you. Crawford had certainly proven that.

As she got off the exit that led to the hospital, she couldn't get rid of the thought that she didn't know there were men who looked like him living in Royal, Texas. Not that she knew all the men in town, mind you. But she figured someone like him would definitely stand out. After all, Royal was a rather small community. And what if she had run into him again, then what?

Nothing.

She didn't have the time or the inclination to get involved with a man. She'd done that in the past and the outcome hadn't been good, which was why she had moved to Royal from Dallas last year. Moving to Royal had meant a fresh start for her. Although, Sheila knew that where she lived was only part of the solution. She had reached the conclusion that a woman didn't need to be involved with a no-good man to have trouble. A woman could do bad all by herself. And she of all people was living proof of that.

Ezekiel Travers chuckled as he watched the attractive woman take off as though she was going to a fire or something. Hell, she wasn't the only one, he thought as he watched her car turn off the interstate at the next exit. Whoever was trying to ruin his best friend, Bradford Price's, reputation had taken things a little too far. According to the phone call he'd received earlier from Brad, the blackmailer had made good on his threat.

Someone had left a baby on the doorstep of the Texas Cattlemen's Club with a note that Brad was the baby's father.

Grabbing his cell phone the moment it began to ring, he knew who the caller was before answering it. "Yeah, Brad?"

"Zeke, where are you?"

"I'm only a few minutes away. And you can believe I'll be getting to the bottom of this."

"I don't know what kind of sick joke someone is trying to play on me, but I swear to you, that baby isn't mine."

Zeke nodded. "And a paternity test can prove that easily, Brad, so calm down."

He had no reason not to believe his best friend about the baby not being his. Brad wouldn't lie about something like that. He and Brad had gotten to be the best of friends while roommates at the University of Texas. After college Brad had returned to Royal to assist in his family's banking empire.

Actually, it had been Brad who suggested Zeke relocate to Royal. He'd made the suggestion during one of their annual all-guys trip to Vegas last year, after Zeke had mentioned his desire to leave Austin and to move to a small town.

Zeke had earned a small fortune and a great reputation as one of the best security consultants in all of Texas. Now he could live anywhere he wanted to, and take his pick of cases.

And it had been Brad who'd connected Zeke with Darius Franklin, another private investigator in Royal who owned a security service and who just happened to be looking for a partner. That had prompted Zeke to fly to Royal. He'd immediately fallen in love with the town and he saw becoming a business partner with Darius a win-win situation. That had been six months ago. When he'd moved to town, he hadn't known that his first case would begin before he could get settled in good, and that his first client would be none other than his best friend.

"I bet Abigail is behind this."

Brad's accusations interrupted Zeke's thoughts. Abigail Langley and Brad were presently in a heated battle to win the presidency of the Texas Cattlemen's Club.

"You have no proof of that and so far I haven't been able to find a link between Ms. Langley and those blackmail letters you've received, Brad. But you can bet if she's connected, I'll expose her. Now, sit tight, I'm on my way."

He clicked off the phone knowing to tell Brad to sit tight was a waste of time. Zeke let out a deep sigh. Brad had begun receiving blackmail letters five months ago. The thought nagged Zeke's mind that maybe if he had been on top of his game and solved the case months ago, it would not have gotten this far and some kid would not have been abandoned at the club.

He of all people knew how that felt. At thirty-three he could still feel the sting of abandonment. Although his own mother hadn't left him on anyone's doorstep, she had left him with her sister and kept on trucking. She hadn't shown up again until sixteen years later. It had been his last year of college and she'd stuck around just long enough to see if he had a chance in the NFL.

He pushed that hurtful time of his life to the back of his mind to concentrate on the problem at hand. If leaving that baby at the TCC with a note claiming she was Brad's kid was supposed to be a joke, then it wasn't funny. And Zeke intended to make sure he and Brad had the last laugh when they exposed the person responsible for such a callous act.

Once Sheila had reached her floor at the hospital, it became evident why they'd called her in. A couple of nurses were out sick and the E.R. was swarming with patients with symptoms ranging from the flu to a man who'd almost lost his finger while chopping down a tree in his front yard. There had also been several minor car accidents.

At least something good had resulted from one of the accidents. A man thinking his girlfriend's injuries were worse than they were, had rushed into the E.R. and proposed. Even Sheila had to admit it had been a very romantic moment. Some women had all the luck.

"So you came in on your off day, uh?"

Sheila glanced at her coworker and smiled. Jill Lanier was a nurse she'd met on her first day at Royal Memorial and they'd become good friends. When she'd moved to Royal she hadn't known a soul, but that had been fine. She was used to being alone. That was the story of her life.

She was about to answer Jill, when the sound of a huge wail stopped her. "What the heck?"

She turned around and saw two police officers walk in carrying a screaming baby. Both she and Jill hurried over to the officers. "What's going on, Officers?" she asked the two men.

One of the officers, the one holding the baby, shook his head. "We don't know why she's crying," he said in frustration. "Someone left her on the doorstep of the Texas Cattlemen's Club and we were told to bring her here."

Sheila had heard all about the Texas Cattlemen's Club, which consisted of a group of men who considered themselves the protectors of Texas, and whose members consisted of the wealthiest men in Texas. One good thing was that the TCC was known to help a number of worthwhile causes in the community. Thanks to them, there was a new cancer wing at the hospital.

Jill took the baby and it only screamed louder. "The TCC? Why would anyone do something like that?"

"Who knows why people abandon their kids," the other officer said. It was apparent he was more than happy to pass the screaming baby on to someone else. However, the infant, who looked to be no more than five months old, was screaming even louder now. Jill, who was a couple of years younger than Sheila and single and carefree, gave them a what-am-I-supposed-to-do-now look as she rocked the baby in her arms.

"And there's a note that's being handed over to Social Services claiming Bradford Price is the father."

Sheila lifted a brow. She didn't know Bradford Price personally, but she had certainly heard of him. His family were blueblood society types. She'd heard they'd made millions in banking.

"Is someone from Social Services on their way here?" Sheila asked, raising her voice to be heard over the crying baby.

"Yes. Price is claiming the baby isn't his. There has to be a paternity test done."

Sheila nodded, knowing that could take a couple of days, possibly even a week.

"And what are we supposed to do with her until then?" Jill asked as she continued to rock the baby in her arms, trying to get her quiet but failing to do so.

"Keep her here," one of the officers responded. He

was backing up, as if he was getting ready to make a run for it. "A woman from Social Services is on her way with everything you'll need. The kid doesn't have a name…at least one wasn't given with the note left with her."

The other officer, the one who'd been carrying the baby, spoke up. "Look, ladies, we have to leave. She threw up on me, so I need to swing by my place and change clothes."

"What about your report?" Sheila called out to the two officers who were rushing off.

"It's completed already and like I said, a woman from Social Services is on her way," the first officer said, before both men quickly exited through the revolving glass doors.

"I can't believe they did that," Jill said with a disgruntled look on her face. "What are we going to do with her? One thing for certain, this kid has a nice set of lungs."

Sheila smiled. "Follow procedure and get her checked out. There might be a medical reason why she's crying. Let's page Dr. Phillips."

"Hey, let me page Dr. Phillips. It's your turn to hold her." Before Sheila could say anything, Jill suddenly plopped the baby in her arms.

"Hey, hey, things can't be that bad, sweetie," Sheila crooned down at the baby as she adjusted her arms to make sure she was holding her right.

Other than the times she worked in the hospital nursery, she'd never held a baby, and rarely came in contact with one. Lois had two kids and was pregnant with another, yet Sheila had only seen her five-year-old niece and three-year-old nephew twice. Her sister had never approved of their father's marriage to Sheila's mother, and Sheila felt she had been the one to pay for it. Lois, who was four years older than Sheila, had been determined never to accept her father's other child. Over the years, Sheila had hoped her attitude toward her would change, but so far it hadn't.

Pushing thoughts of Lois from her mind, Sheila continued to smile down at the baby. And as if on cue the little girl stared up at Sheila with the most gorgeous pair of hazel eyes, and suddenly stopped crying. In fact, she smiled, showing dimples in both cheeks.

Sheila couldn't help chuckling. "What are you laughing at, baby-doll? Do I look funny or something?" She was rewarded with another huge smile from the baby. "You're such a pretty little thing, all bright and full of sunshine. I think I'll call you Sunnie until we find out your real name."

"Dr. Phillips is on his way and I'm needed on the fourth floor," Jill said, making a dash toward the elevator. "How did you get her to stop crying, Sheila?" she asked before stepping on the elevator.

Sheila shrugged and glanced back at the baby, who was still smiling up at her. "I guess she likes me."

"Apparently she does," a deep, husky male voice said from behind them.

Sheila turned around and her gaze collided with the most gorgeous set of brown eyes she'd ever seen on a man. They were bedroom eyes. The kind that brought to mind silken sheets and passion. But this wasn't the first time she had looked into those same eyes.

She immediately knew where she'd seen them before as her gaze roamed over his features. Recognition appeared in his gaze the moment it hit hers as well. Standing before her, looking sexier than any man had a right to look, was the guy who'd been in the car next to hers at the traffic light. He was the man who'd given her a flirtatious smile before she'd deliberately sped off to ditch him.

Evidently that hadn't done any good, since he was here, standing before her in vivid living color.

Two

This was the second time today he'd seen this woman, Zeke thought. Just as before, he thought she looked good…even wearing scrubs. Nothing could hide the wavy black hair that came to her shoulders, the light brown eyes and luscious café-au-lait skin.

He wondered if anyone ever told her she could be a very delicious double for actress Sanaa Lathan. The woman before him was just a tad shorter than the actress, but in his book she was just as curvy. And she was a nurse. Hell, she could take his temperature any time and any place. He could even suggest she take it now, because there was no doubt in his mind looking at her was making it rise.

"May I help you?"

He blinked and swallowed deeply. "Yes, that baby you're holding…"

She narrowed her eyes and clutched the baby closer to her breast in a protective stance. "Yes, what about her?"

"I want to find out everything there is about her," he said.

She lifted an arched brow. "And you are…?"

He gave what he hoped was a charming smile. "Zeke Travers, private investigator."

Sheila opened her mouth to speak, when a deep, male voice intruded behind her. "Zeke Travers! Son of a gun! With Brad Price as quarterback, you as split end and Chris Richards as wide receiver, that was UT's best football season. I recall them winning a national championship title that year. Those other teams didn't stand a chance with you three. Someone mentioned you had moved to Royal."

She then watched as Dr. Warren Phillips gave the man a huge bear hug. Evidently they knew each other, and as she listened further, she was finding out quite a lot about the handsome stranger.

"Yes, I moved to town six months ago," Zeke was saying. "Austin was getting too big for me. I've decided to try small-town life for a while. Brad convinced me Royal was the place," he said, grinning. "And I was able to convince Darius Franklin he needed a partner."

"So you joined forces with Darius over at Global Securities?"

"Yes, and things are working out great so far. Darius is a good man and I really like this town. In fact, I like it more and more each day." His gaze then shifted to her and her gaze locked with his as it had done that morning.

The clearing of Dr. Phillips's throat reminded them they weren't alone.

"So, what brings you to Royal Memorial, Zeke?" Dr. Phillips asked, and it was evident to Sheila that Dr. Phillips had picked up on the man's interest in her.

"That baby she's holding. It was left abandoned at

the TCC today with a note claiming Brad's the father. And I intend to prove that he's not."

"In that case," Dr. Phillips said, "I think we need to go into that private examination room over there and check this baby out."

A short while later Dr. Phillips slid his stethoscope into the pocket of his lab coat as he leaned back against the table. "Well, this young lady is certainly in good health."

He chuckled and then added, "And she certainly refused to let anyone hold her other than you, Nurse Hopkins. If you hadn't been present and within her reach, it would have been almost impossible for me to examine her."

Sheila laughed as she held the baby to her while glancing down at the infant. "She's beautiful. I can't imagine anyone wanting to abandon her."

"Well, it happened," Zeke said.

A tingling sensation rode up her spine with the comment and she was reminded that Zeke Travers was in the examination room with them. It was as if he refused to let the baby out of his sight.

She turned slightly. "What makes you so sure she's not Bradford Price's child, Mr. Travers? I recall running into Mr. Price a time or two and he also has hazel eyes."

He narrowed his gaze. "So do a million other people in this country, Ms. Hopkins."

Evidently he didn't like being questioned about the possibility. So she turned to Dr. Phillips. "Did that social worker who came by while you were examining the baby say what will happen to Sunnie?" she asked.

Dr. Phillips lifted a brow. "Sunnie?"

"Yes," Sheila said, smiling. "I thought she was a

vision of sunshine the moment I looked at her. And since no one knows her name I thought Sunnie would fit. Sounds better than Jane Doe," she added.

"I agree," Dr. Phillips said, chuckling. "And the social worker, Ms. Talbert, is as baffled as everyone else, especially since Brad says the baby isn't his."

"She's not his," Zeke said, inserting himself into the conversation again. "Brad's been receiving blackmail letters for five months now, threatening to do something like this unless he paid up."

Zeke rubbed the back of his neck. "I told him to ignore the letters while I looked into it. I honestly didn't think the person would carry out their threats if Brad didn't pay up. Evidently, I was wrong."

And that's what continued to bother him the most, Zeke thought as he glanced over at the baby. He should have nipped this nasty business in the bud long ago. And what Ms. Hopkins said was true, because he'd noted it himself. The baby had hazel eyes, and not only were they hazel, they were the same shade of hazel as Brad's.

He'd asked Brad if there was any chance the baby could be his, considering the fact Brad was a known playboy. But after talking to Brad before coming over here, and now that he knew the age of the baby, Zeke was even more convinced Brad wasn't the father. Warren had confirmed the baby's age as five months and Brad had stated he hadn't slept with any woman over the past eighteen months.

"To answer your question, Nurse Hopkins," Dr. Phillips said, breaking into Zeke's thoughts, "Ms. Talbert wants to wait to see what the paternity test reveals. I agreed that we can keep the baby here until then."

"Here?"

"Yes, that would be best until the test results comes back, that is unless Brad has a problem participating in the test," Dr. Phillips said, glancing over at Zeke.

"Brad knows that it's for the best, and he will cooperate any way he can," Zeke acknowledged.

"But it doesn't seem fair for Sunnie to have to stay here at the hospital. She's in perfect health," Sheila implored. "Ms. Talbert has indicated the test results might take two weeks to come back."

She then glared over at Zeke. "Whether the baby is officially his or not, I would think your client would want the best for Sunnie until her parentage is proven or disproven."

Zeke crossed his arms over his chest. "So what do you suggest, Ms. Hopkins? I agree staying here isn't ideal for the baby, but the only other option is for her to get turned over to Social Services. If that happens she'll go into foster care and will get lost in the system when it's proven my client is *not* her father."

Sheila nibbled on her bottom lip, not having a response to give him. She glanced down at the baby she held in her arms. For whatever reason, Sunnie's mother hadn't wanted her and it didn't seem fair for her to suffer because of it. She knew how it felt not to be wanted.

"I might have an idea that might work, Nurse Hopkins, granted you agree to go along with it," Dr. Phillips said. "And I'll have to get Ms. Talbert to agree to it, as well."

"Yes?" she said, wondering what his idea was.

"A few years ago the wife of one of my colleagues, Dr. Webb, was hit with a similar incident when someone left a baby on her doorstep before they were married. Because Winona grew up in foster care herself, she hadn't wanted the baby to end up the same way. To make a long story short, Winona and Dr. Webb ended up marrying and keeping the baby to make sure it didn't get lost in the system."

Sheila nodded. "So what are you suggesting?"

Dr. Phillips smiled. "That you become Sunnie's emergency foster parent until everything is resolved. I believe I'll be able to convince Ms. Talbert to go along with it, and given the fact the Prices are huge benefactors to this hospital, as well as to a number of other nonprofit organizations, I think it would be in everyone's best interest that the baby's welfare remain a top priority."

Sheila looked shocked. "Me? A foster parent! I wouldn't know what to do with a baby."

"You couldn't convince me of that, Ms. Hopkins. The baby won't let anyone else touch her and you seem to be a natural with her," Zeke said, seeing the merits of what Dr. Phillips proposed. "Besides, you're a nurse, someone who is used to taking care of people."

Although Brad swore the baby wasn't his, he would still be concerned with the baby's health and safety until everything was resolved. And what Zeke just said was true. He thought the woman was a natural with the baby, and the baby had gotten totally attached to her. He had a feeling Ms. Hopkins was already sort of attached to the baby, as well.

"And if you're concerned as to how you'd be able to handle both your job and the baby, I propose that the hospital agrees to give you a leave of absence during the time that the child is in your care. My client will be more than happy to replace your salary," Zeke said.

"I think that would be an excellent idea," Warren said. "One I think I could push past the chief of staff.

The main thing everyone should be concerned about is Sunnie's well-being."

Sheila couldn't help agreeing. But her? A foster parent? "How long do you think I'll have to take care of her?" she asked, looking down at Sunnie, who was still smiling up at her.

"No more than a couple of weeks, if even that long," Zeke said. "The results of the paternity test should be back by then and we'll know how to proceed."

Sheila nibbled her bottom lip, when Sunnie reached and grabbed hold of a lock of her hair, seemingly forcing Sheila to look down at her—into her beautiful hazel eyes, while she made a lot of cheerful baby sounds. At that moment Sheila knew she would do it. Sunnie needed a temporary home and she would provide her with one. It was the least she could do, and deep down she knew it was something that she wanted to do. This was the first time she'd felt someone truly, really needed her.

She glanced up at both men to see they were patiently waiting for her answer. She drew in a deep breath. "Yes. I would be happy to be Sunnie's emergency foster parent."

After removing his jacket, Zeke slid into the seat of his car and leaned back as he gazed at the entrance to the hospital. He felt good about Sheila Hopkins agreeing to take on the role of foster parent. That way he would know the baby was being well cared for while he turned up the heat on the investigation to clear Brad's name.

He intended to pursue each and every lead. He would not leave a stone, no matter how small, unturned. He intended to get this potential scandal under total control before it could go any further.

Now if he could control his attraction to Sheila

Hopkins. The woman was definitely temptation with a capital T. Being in close quarters with her, even with Warren in the room, had been pure torture. She was a looker, but it was clear she didn't see herself that way, and he couldn't help wondering, why not? He hadn't seen a ring on her finger and, when he'd hung back to speak with Warren in private, the only thing his friend could tell him was that she was a model employee, caring to a fault, dependable and intelligent.

Warren had also verified she was single and had moved from Dallas last year. But still, considering everything, Zeke felt it wouldn't hurt to do a background check on her, just to be on the safe side. The last thing he wanted was for her to be someone who'd be tempted to sell this story to the tabloids. That was the last thing Brad needed. His best friend was depending on him to bring an end to this nightmare, and he would.

Zeke was about to turn the ignition in his car, when he glanced through the windshield to see Sheila Hopkins. She was walking quickly across the parking lot to the car he had seen her in that morning. She looked as if she was dashing off to fight a fire. Curious as to where she could be going in such a hurry, he got out of the car, walked swiftly to cross the parking lot and intercepted her before she could reach her vehicle.

She nearly yelled in fright when he stepped in front of her. "What do you think you're doing?" she asked, covering her heart with the palm of her hand. "You just scared me out of my wits."

"Sorry, but I saw you tearing across the parking lot. What's the hurry?"

Sheila drew a deep breath to get her heart beating back normal in her chest. She looked up at Zeke Travers and couldn't do anything about her stomach doing flips.

It had been hard enough while in the examination room to stop her gaze from roaming all over him every chance it got.

"I'm leaving Sunnie in the hospital tonight while I go pick up the things I'll need for her. I'm going to need a baby bed, diapers, clothes and all kinds of other items. I plan on shopping today and come back for her first thing in the morning once my house is ready."

She paused a moment. "I hated leaving her. She started crying. I feel like I'm abandoning her."

A part of Zeke was relieved to know she was a woman who would feel some sort of guilt in abandoning a child. His own mother had not. He drew in a deep breath as he remembered what Sheila Hopkins had said about needing to go shopping for all that baby stuff. He hadn't thought of the extra expenses taking on a baby would probably cost her.

"Let me go with you to pick up the stuff. That way I can pay for it."

She raised a brow. "Why would you want to do that?"

"Because whether or not Brad's the father—which he's not—he wants the baby taken care of and is willing to pay for anything she might need." He hadn't discussed it with Brad, but knew there wouldn't be a problem. Brad was concerned for the baby's welfare.

She seemed to be studying his features as if she was trying to decide if he was serious, Zeke thought. And then she asked, "You sure? I have to admit that I hadn't worked all the baby expenses into my weekly budget, but if I need to get money out of my savings then I—"

"No, that won't be necessary and Brad wouldn't want it any other way and like I said, I'll be glad to go with you and help."

Sheila felt a tingling sensation in the pit of her

stomach. The last thing she needed was Zeke Travers in her presence too long. "No, I'll be able to manage things, but I appreciate the offer."

"No, really, I insist. Why wouldn't you want me to help? I'll provide you with two extra hands."

That wasn't all he would be providing her with, she thought, looking at him. Besides the drop-dead gorgeous looks, at some point he had taken off his jacket to reveal the width of his shoulders beneath his white dress shirt. She also noticed the way his muscular thighs fit into a pair of dress slacks.

"We could leave your car here. I have a feeling you'll want to come back and check on the baby later. We can go in my vehicle," he added before she could respond to what he'd said.

She lifted a brow. "You have a two-seater."

He chuckled. "Yes, but I also have a truck. And that's what you're going to need to haul something as big as a box containing a baby bed. And in order to haul the kid away from here you're going to need a car seat tomorrow."

Sheila tilted her head back and drew in a deep breath. Had she bit off more than she could chew? She hadn't thought of all that. She needed to make a list and not work off the top of her head. And he was right about her needing a truck and wanting to return tonight to check on Sunnie. The sound of her crying had followed Sheila all the way to the elevator. She hated leaving her, but she had to prepare her house for Sunnie's visit.

"Ms. Hopkins?"

She looked back at Zeke Travers. "Fine, Mr. Travers, I'll accept your generosity. If you're sure it's not going out of your way."

He smiled. "I'm not going out of my way, I assure

you. Like I said, Brad would want what's best for the baby even if she isn't his."

She arched a brow. "You certainly seem so sure of that."

"I am. Now, it's going to be my job in addition to making sure the baby is safe and well cared for, to find out who's trying to nail him with this and to clear his name."

Zeke paused a moment and stared down at her. "And speaking of names, I suggest you call me Zeke, instead of Mr. Travers."

She smiled. "Why, is Mr. Travers what they call your father?"

"I wouldn't know."

Sheila's heart skipped a beat when she realized what he'd said and what he'd meant by saying it. "I'm sorry, I didn't mean anything. The last guy who told me not to call him by his last name said the reason was that's what people called his daddy."

"No harm done, and I hope you don't mind if I call you Sheila."

"No, I don't mind."

"Good. Come on, Sheila, my car is parked over here," he said.

Sheila felt her stomach twist in all kinds of knots when she heard her name flow from his lips. And as she walked beside Zeke across the parking lot, a number of misgivings flooded her mind. For one thing, she wasn't sure what role he intended to play with her becoming Sunnie's foster parent. She understood Bradford Price was his client and he intended to clear the man's name. But she had to think beyond that. If Bradford wasn't Sunnie's father then who was? Where was the mother and why had the baby been abandoned with a note claiming Bradford was the father when he said he wasn't?

There were a lot of questions and she had a feeling the man walking beside her intended to have answers for all of them soon enough. She also had a feeling he was the sort of person who got things accomplished when he set his mind to it. And she could tell he intended to investigate this case to the fullest.

His main concern might be on his friend, but hers was on Sunnie. What would happen to her if it was proven Bradford wasn't the child's father? Would the man cease caring about Sunnie's welfare? Would it matter to him that she would then become just a statistic in the system?

He might not care, but she would, and at that moment she vowed to protect Sunnie any way she could.

Three

While they were on their way to the store to pick up items for the baby, Sheila clicked off the phone and sighed deeply as she glanced over at Zeke. "I just talked to one of the nurses in Pediatrics. Sunnie cried herself to sleep," she said.

There was no need telling him that she knew just how that felt. She was reminded of how many nights as a child she had lain in bed and cried herself to sleep because her mother was too busy trying to catch the next rich husband to spend any time with her. And her father, once he'd discovered what a gold digger Cassie Hopkins was, he hadn't wasted time moving out and taking Lois with him and leaving her behind.

"That's good to hear, Sheila," Zeke responded.

There was another tingling sensation in the pit of her stomach. She couldn't help it. It did something to her each and every time he pronounced her name. He said it with a deep Texas drawl that could send shivers all through her.

"So how long have you been living in Royal?" he asked.

She glanced over at him. "A year." She knew from his conversation with Dr. Phillips that he had moved to town six months ago, so there was no need to ask him that. She also knew he'd come from Austin because he wanted to try living in a small city.

"You like it here?"

She nodded. "So far. The people are nice, but I spend a lot of my time at the hospital, so I still haven't met all my neighbors, only those next door."

She switched her gaze off him to look out the window at the homes and stores they passed. What she decided not to add was that other than working, and occasional trips to the market, she rarely left home. The people at the hospital had become her family

Now that she'd agreed to a fourteen-day leave of absence, she would have her hands full caring for Sunnie, and a part of her actually looked forward to that.

"You're smiling."

She glanced back at him. Did the man notice every single thing? "Is it a crime?"

He chuckled. "No."

The deep, husky rumble of his chuckle sent shivers sweeping through her again. And because she couldn't help herself, when the car came to a stop at the traffic light she glanced back over at him and then wished she hadn't done so. The slow smile that suddenly curved his lips warmed her all over.

"Now you're the one smiling," she pointed out.

"And is that a crime?"

Grinning, she shook her head. He'd made her see just how ridiculous her response to him had been. "No, it's not."

"Good. Because if I get arrested, Sheila, so do you. And it would be my request that we get put in the same jail cell."

She told herself not to overreact to what he'd said. Of course he would try to flirt with her. He was a man. She'd gotten hit on by a number of doctors at the hospital as well as several police officers around town. Eventually, they found out what Zeke would soon discover. It was a waste of their time. She had written men off. When it came to the opposite sex, she preferred her space. The only reason she was with him now was because of Sunnie. She considered Zeke Travers as a means to an end.

When he exited off the expressway and moments later turned into a nice gated community, she was in awe of the large and spacious ranch-style homes that sat on at least thirty acres of land. She had heard about the Cascades, the section of Royal where the wealthy lived. He evidently was doing well in the P.I. business. "You live in this community?" she asked.

"Yes. I came from Austin on an apartment-hunting trip and ended up purchasing a house instead. I always wanted a lot of land and to own horses and figured buying in here was a good investment."

She could just imagine, especially with the size of the ranch house whose driveway they were pulling into. The house had to be sitting almost six hundred or more feet back off the road. She could see a family of twelve living here and thought the place was definitely too large for just one person.

"How many acres is this?" she asked.

"Forty. I needed that much with the horses."

"How many do you own?"

"Twelve now, but I plan to expand. I've hired several ranch hands to help me take care of things. And I ride every chance I get. What about you? Do you ride?"

She thought of her mother's second and third husbands. They had owned horses and required that she know how to ride. "Yes, I know how to ride."

He glanced at his watch. "It won't take me long to switch vehicles," he said, bringing the car to a stop. "You're invited in if you like and you're welcome to look around."

"No, I'll be fine waiting out here until you return," she said.

He got out of the car and turned to her and smiled. "I don't bite, you know."

"Trust me, Zeke, if for one minute I thought you did, I wouldn't be here."

"So you think I'm harmless?" he asked, grinning.

"Not harmless but manageable. I'm sure all your focus will be on trying to figure out who wants to frame your friend. You don't have time for anything else."

He flashed a sexy smile. "Don't be so sure of that, Sheila Hopkins." He closed the door and she watched as he strolled up the walkway to his front door, thinking his walk was just as sexy as his smile.

Zeke unlocked his door and pushed it open. He had barely made it inside his house when the phone rang. Closing the door behind him, he pulled his cell phone off the clip on his belt. He checked the caller ID. "Yes, Brad?"

"You didn't call. How was the baby?"

Zeke leaned up against the wall supporting the staircase. "She's fine, but she cries a lot."

"I noticed. And no one could get her to stop. Did they check her out to make sure nothing is wrong with her?"

Zeke smiled. "She was checked out. Just so happens that Warren Phillips was on duty and he's the one who gave her a clean bill of health, although she still wanted to prove to everyone what a good set of lungs she had."

"I'm glad she's okay. I was worried about her."

Zeke nodded. "Are you sure there's nothing you want to tell me? I did happen to notice the kid does have your eyes."

"Don't get cute, Zeke. The kid isn't mine. But she's just a baby and I can't help worrying about her."

"Hey, man, I was just kidding, and I understand. I can't help worrying about her, too. But we might have found a way where we don't have to worry about her while I delve into my investigation."

"And what way is that?"

"That way happens to be a nurse who works at Royal Memorial by the name of Sheila Hopkins. She's the only one who can keep the baby quiet. It's the weirdest thing. The kid screams at everyone else, but she's putty in Sheila Hopkins's hands. She actually smiles instead of crying."

"You're kidding."

"No, I saw her smile myself. Warren suggested that Sheila keep Sunnie for the time being," Zeke explained.

"Sunnie?"

"Yes, that's the name Sheila gave the kid for now. She said it sounded better than Jane Doe and I agree."

There was a slight pause and then Brad asked, "And this Sheila Hopkins agreed to do it?"

"Yes, until the results of the paternity test come back, so the sooner you can do your part the better."

"I've made an appointment to have it done tomorrow."

"Good. And I'm going shopping with Sheila for baby stuff. She's single and doesn't have any kids of her own, so she'll need all new stuff, which I'm billing you for, by the way."

"Fine." There was a pause, and then Brad said, "I was thinking that perhaps it would be best if I hired a nanny and keep the baby instead of—"

"Hold up. Don't even consider it. We don't want anyone seeing your kindness as an admission of guilt, Brad. The next thing everyone will think is that the baby is really yours."

"Yes, but what do you know about this nurse? You said she's single. She might be pretty good at taking care of patients, but are you sure she knows how to take care of a baby?"

"I'm not sure about anything regarding Sheila Hopkins, other than what Warren told me. She's worked at the hospital about a year. But don't worry, I've already taken measures to have her checked out. Roy is doing a thorough background check on Sheila Hopkins as we speak."

Suddenly Zeke heard a noise behind him and turned around. Sheila was leaning against his door with her arms crossed over her chest. The look on her face let him know she had heard some, if not all, of his conversation with Brad and wasn't happy about it.

"Brad, I need to go. I'll call you back later." He then hung up the phone.

Before he could open his mouth, Sheila placed her hands on her hips and narrowed her eyes at him. "Please take me back to the hospital to get my car. There's no way I'm going anywhere with a man who doesn't trust me."

Then she turned and walked out the door and slammed it shut behind her.

Sheila was halfway down the walkway, when Zeke ran behind her and grabbed her arm. "Let me go," she said and angrily snatched it back.

"We need to talk and I prefer we don't do it out here," Zeke said.

She glared up at him. "And I prefer we don't do it anywhere. I have nothing to say to you. How dare you have me investigated like I'm some sort of criminal."

"I never said you were a criminal."

"Then why the background check, Zeke?"

He rubbed his hands down his face. "I'm a P.I., Sheila. I investigate people. Nothing personal, but think about it. Sunnie will be in your care for two weeks. I don't know you personally and I need to know she's not only in a safe environment but with someone both Brad and I can trust. Would you not want me to check out the person whose care she's been placed in?"

Sheila sighed deeply, knowing that she would. "But I'd never do anything to harm her."

"I believe that, but I have to make sure. All I'm doing is a basic background check to make certain you don't have any past criminal history." After a moment he said, "Come on in, let's talk inside."

She thought about his request then decided it might be best if they did talk inside after all. She had a tendency to raise her voice when she was angry about something.

"Fine." She stalked off ahead of him.

* * *

By the time Zeke followed her inside the house, she was in the middle of the living room pacing, and he could tell she was still mad. He quietly closed the door behind him and leaned against it, folding his arms across his chest, with one booted heel over the other, as he watched her. Again he was struck by just how beautiful she was.

For some reason he was more aware of it now than before. There was fire in her eyes, annoyance in her steps, and the way she was unconsciously swaying her hips was downright sensual. She had taken center stage, was holding it and he was a captive audience of one.

Then she stopped pacing and placed her hands on her hips to face him. She glared him down. The woman could not have been more than five-four at the most. Yet even with his height of six-four she was making him feel shorter. Damn. He hadn't meant for her to overhear his conversation with Brad. Hadn't she told him she hadn't wanted to come in?

"You were supposed to stay outside. You said you didn't want to come in," he blurted out for some reason.

He watched as she stiffened her spine even more. "And that gave you the right to talk about me?"

His heart thudded deeply in his chest. The last thing he had time or the inclination to do was deal with an emotional female. "Look, Sheila, like I said before, I am a private investigator. My job is to know people and I don't like surprises. Anyone who comes in contact with the baby for any long period of time will get checked out by me."

He rubbed his hand down his face and released a frustrated sigh. "Look. It's not that I was intentionally questioning your character. I was mainly assuring my client that a child that someone is claiming to be his has been placed in the best of care until the issue is resolved by way of a paternity test. There's no reason for you to take it personally. It's not about you. It's about Sunnie. Had you been the president's mother-in-law I'd still do a background check. My client is a very wealthy man and my job is to protect him at all costs, which is why I intend to find out who is behind this."

He paused for a moment. "You do want what's best for Sunnie, don't you?"

"Of course."

"So do I, and so does Brad. That baby was abandoned, and the last thing I would want is for her not to have some stability in her life over the next couple of weeks. She deserves that at least. Neither of us know what will happen after that."

His words gave Sheila pause and deflated her anger somewhat. Although she didn't want to admit it, what he said was true. It wasn't about her but about Sunnie. She should be everyone's main concern. Background checks were routine and she would have expected that one be done if they'd hired a nanny for Sunnie. She didn't know Zeke like he didn't know her, and with that suspicious mind of his—which came with the work he did—he would want to check her out regardless of the fact that Dr. Phillips had spoken highly of her. But that didn't mean she had to like the fact Zeke had done it.

"Fine," she snapped. "You've done your job. Now, take me back to the hospital so I can get my car."

"We're going shopping for the baby stuff as planned, Sheila. You still need my truck, so please put your emotions aside and agree to do what's needed to be done."

"Emotions!" Before thinking about it, she quickly crossed the room to stand in front of him.

"Yes, emotions."

His voice had lowered and he reached out and tilted her chin up. "Has anyone ever told you how sexy you look when you're angry?"

And before she could take another breath, he lowered his mouth to hers.

Why did her lips have to be so soft?
Why did she have to taste so darn good?
And why wasn't she resisting him?

Those questions rammed through Zeke's mind as his heart banged brutally in his chest at the feel of his mouth on Sheila's. He pushed those questions and others to the back of his mind as he deepened the kiss, took it to another level—although his senses were telling him that was the last thing he needed to do.

He didn't heed their advice. Instead, he wrapped his arms around Sheila's waist to bring her closer to the fit of him as he feasted on her mouth. He knew he wasn't the only one affected by the kiss when he felt her hardened nipples pressing into his chest. He could tell she hadn't gotten kissed a lot, at least not to this degree, and she seemed unsure of herself, but he remedied that by taking control. She moaned and he liked the sound of it and definitely like the feel of her plastered against him.

He could go on kissing her for hours…days…months. The very thought gave him pause and he gradually pulled his mouth from hers. Hours, days and months meant an involvement with a woman and he didn't do involvements. He did casual affairs and nothing more. And the last thing he did was mix business with pleasure.

* * *

Sheila's first coherent thought after Zeke released her lips was that she had never, not even in her wildest dreams, been kissed like that. She still felt tingling in her toes and her entire body; her every limb and muscle felt like pure jelly, which was probably the reason she was quivering like the dickens inside.

She slowly drew air into her lungs, held it a moment before slowly letting it out. She could still taste him on her tongue. How had he gotten so entrenched there? She quickly answered her own question when she remembered how his tongue had taken hold of hers, mated with it and sucked on it.

She muttered a couple colorful expletives under her breath when she gazed up at him. She should not have allowed him to kiss her like that. She'd be the first to admit she had enjoyed it, but still. The eyes staring back at her were dark and heated as if he wanted a repeat performance. She cleared her throat. "Why did you kiss me?"

Why had he kissed her? Zeke asked himself that same question as he took a step back. He needed to put distance between them or else he would be tempted to kiss her again.

"You were talking," he said, grabbing the first excuse he could think of.

"No, I wasn't."

He lifted a brow. Hadn't she been? He tried to backtrack and recall just what was taking place between them before she'd stormed across the room to get in his face. When he remembered, he shrugged. "Doesn't matter. You would have said something you regretted and I decided to wipe the words off your lips."

Sheila frowned. "I suggest that you don't ever do it again."

That slow, sexy smile that she'd seen earlier returned, and instead of saying he wouldn't kiss her again, he crossed his arms over his chest and asked, "So, what brought you inside? You said you were going to wait outside."

He had changed subjects and she decided to follow his lead. "Your car began beeping loudly as if it was going to blow up or something."

His smile widened to emphasize the dimples in his cheek. "That's my fax machine. It's built into my console in a way that's not detectable."

She shook her head. "What are you, a regular James Bond?"

"No. Bond is a secret agent. I'm a private investigator. There's a big difference." He glanced at his watch. "If you're ready, we can leave. My truck is this way."

"What about the fax that was coming through?"

"I have a fax in the truck as well. It will come in on both."

"Oh."

She followed him through a spacious dining room and kitchen that was stylishly decorated. The living room was also fashionably furnished. Definitely more so than hers. "You have a nice home."

"Thanks, and if you're talking about the furniture and decorating, I can't take credit. It was a model home and I bought it as is. I saw it. I liked it. I got it."

He saw it, he liked it and he got it. She wondered if that was how he operated with everything in his life.

"Where do you want me to put these boxes?" Zeke asked, carrying two under his arms. One contained a baby car seat and the other a baby bath. He hadn't wanted to tell her, but he thought instead of purchasing just the basics that she'd gotten carried away. The kid would only be with her for two weeks at the most, not two years.

"You can set them down anywhere. I'm going to stay up late tonight putting stuff up."

After placing the boxes in a corner of the room, he glanced around. The place was small, but it suited her. Her furniture was nice and her two-story home was neat as a pin. He could imagine how it was going to look with baby stuff cluttering it up.

"I'm going to call the hospital again to check on Sunnie."

He bit down on his lips, forcing back a reminder that she had called the hospital less than an hour ago. And before that, while they had been shopping in Target for all the items on her list, she had called several times then as well. It was a good thing she knew the nurses taking care of the baby, otherwise they would probably consider her a nuisance.

While she was on the phone, he went back outside to get more boxes out of the truck. Although she didn't live in a gated community, it was in a nice section of town, and he felt good about that. And he noticed she had an alarm system, but he would check the locks on her doors anyway. Until he discovered the identity of the person who'd tried to extort money from Brad, he wasn't taking any chances. What if the blackmailer tried to kidnap the baby back?

He had made several trips back and forth into the house before Sheila had finally gotten off the phone. He glanced over at her. "Is anything wrong?"

She shook her head. "No. Sunnie awakened for a short while, but she's gone back to sleep now."

Hell, he should hope so. He glanced at his watch. It was after nine o'clock. He should know since they'd closed the store. He figured that kid should be asleep by now. Didn't she have a bedtime?

"Okay, all the boxes are in, what do you need me to do now?"

Sheila glanced over at him, tempted to tell him what he could do was leave. He was unnerving her. He'd done so while they'd been shopping for the baby items. There was something about a good-looking man that could get to a woman each and every time, and she'd gotten her share with him today. Several times while walking down the aisles of the store, they had brushed against each other, and although both had tried downplaying the connection, she'd felt it and knew he'd felt it as well. And he smelled good. Most of the men at the hospital smelled sanitized. She was reminded of a real man's scent while around him. And then there was that kiss she was trying hard to forget. However, she was finding it difficult to do so each and every time she looked at his lips. His mouth had certainly done a number on her.

She thought every woman should spend the day shopping with a man for baby items at least once in her lifetime. Sheila couldn't help remembering the number of times they'd needed assistance from a store clerk. Finally, they'd been assigned their own personal clerk, probably to get them out the store sooner. She was sure the employees wanted to go home at some point that night. And she couldn't forget how the clerk assumed they were married, although neither of them was wearing a wedding ring. Go figure.

"You can take me to get my car now," she said,

tucking a loose lock of hair behind her ear and trying not to stare at him. She shouldn't be surprised that he practically dominated her living room by standing in the middle of it. Everything else seemed to fade to black. He was definitely the main attraction with his height, muscular build and overall good looks.

"What about the baby bed?"

She quirked a brow. "What about it?"

"When are you going to put it together?"

She nibbled on her bottom lip, thinking that was a good question. It was one of the largest items she'd purchased and the clerk had turned down her offer to buy the one on display. That certainly would have made things easier for her. Instead, he'd sold her one in a box that included instructions that would probably look like Greek to her.

"Later tonight."

A smile curved his lips. "I should hope so if you plan on bringing the baby home tomorrow."

She wrapped her arms around herself. She hadn't told him yet, but she planned on bringing Sunnie home tonight. It was getting so bad with her crying that the nurses hated it when she woke up. Her crying would wake all the other babies. She had talked to the head nurse, who would be contacting Dr. Phillips to make sure Sunnie could be released into her care and custody tonight. She was just waiting for a callback.

Zeke studied Sheila. Maybe his brain was over-reacting, but he had a feeling she was keeping something from him. Maybe it was because she was giving a lot away. Like the way she had wrapped her arms around herself. Or the nervous look in her eyes. Or it could be the way she was nibbling on the lips he'd kissed earlier that day. A kiss he wished he could forget but couldn't. For some reason his mouth had felt right locked to hers.

He crossed his arms over his chest. "Is there something you want to tell me?"

She dropped her arms to her sides. "Sunnie is keeping the other babies up."

That didn't surprise him. He'd heard the kid cry. She had a good set of lungs. "She's sleeping now, right?"

"Yes, but as you know, she probably won't sleep through the night."

No, he didn't know that. "Why not?"

"Most babies don't. That's normal. The older they get the longer they will sleep through the night. In Sunnie's case, she probably sleeps a lot during the day and is probably up for at least part of the night."

"And you're prepared for that?"

"I have to be."

It occurred to him the sacrifices she would be making. His concentration had been so focused on the baby, he hadn't thought about the changes keeping Sunnie would make in her life. When she'd been on the phone and he'd been hauling in the boxes, he had taken a minute to pull his fax. It had been the background check on her. The firm he used was thorough and he'd held her life history in his hand while holding that one sheet of paper.

She was twenty-seven and every hospital she'd worked in since college had given her a glowing recommendation. She was a law-abiding citizen. Had never even received a speeding ticket. One year she had even received a medal for heroism from the Dallas Fire Department because she'd rushed inside a burning house to help save an elderly man, and then provided him with medical services until paramedics got there. That unselfish act had made national news.

On a more personal side, he knew she had a sister whom she didn't visit often. She had a mother whom she visited once or twice a year. Her mother was divorced from husband number five, a CEO of a resort in Florida. Her father had died five years ago. Her only sister, who was four years older, was from her father's first marriage. Sheila had been the product of the old man's second marriage.

"Tell me what else I can do to help," he said.

She released a deep sigh. "I want to bring Sunnie here tonight. The nurses are contacting Dr. Phillips for his approval. I hope to get a call from him any minute. Either way, whether I get Sunnie tonight or tomorrow, I'll need the bed, so if you really don't mind, I'd appreciate it if you would put it together. I'm not good at doing stuff like that."

He nodded. "No problem." He began rolling up his sleeves. "You wouldn't happen to have a beer handy, would you?"

She smiled. "Yes, I'll go grab one for you."

And then she took off and he was left standing while wondering why he couldn't stop thinking about the time he had kissed her.

"We're glad you're here," one of the nurses in Pediatrics said anxiously. "We have her packed up and ready to go," she added, smiling brightly.

"She's been expressing herself again, eh?" Zeke asked, chuckling.

Sheila glanced over at Zeke, wondering why he was there. It hadn't taken him any time to put up the baby bed, and he'd taken the time to help with the other things as well. Except for the fact Sunnie was a girl and the room was painted blue, everything else was perfect. By the time they'd left, it had looked like a genuine nursery and she couldn't wait for Sunnie to see it.

That brought her back to the question she'd wondered about earlier. Why was he here? She figured he would drop her off and keep moving. She had a baby car seat, so as far as she was concerned, she was ready to go. But she couldn't dismiss the nervous tension in her stomach.

Sunnie had clung to her earlier today when the police officers had first brought her in. What if she no longer had that attachment to her and treated her like the others and continue to cry all over the place? She drew in a deep breath, wanting to believe that that special connection between them was still there.

"Where is she?" she asked the nurse.

"Down that hall. Trust me, you'll hear her as soon as you clear the waiting area. You won't be able to miss it. All of us are wearing homemade earplugs."

Sheila knew the nurse had said it as a joke, but she didn't see anything funny. She was ready to get Sunnie and go home. Home. Already she was thinking of her place as the baby's home. Before tonight, to her it was just a place to eat and sleep. Now, taking Sunnie there had her thinking differently.

True to what the nurse had said, Sunnie could be heard the moment Sheila and Zeke passed the waiting room. He put his hand on her arm for them to stop walking. He studied her features. "What's wrong? Why are you so tense?"

How had he known? She released a nervous sigh. "I've been gone over eight hours. What if Sunnie isn't attached to me anymore? What if she sees me and continues to cry?"

Zeke stared at her. The answer seemed quite obvious to him. It didn't matter. The kid was going home with her regardless. But he could see it was important for this encounter with the baby not to constitute a rejection. He wondered why he cared. He reached out and took her hand in his and began rubbing it when it felt cold.

"Hey, she's going to remember you. She liked you too much not to. If you recall, I was here when she was clinging to you like you were her lifeline, her protector and the one person she thinks is there for her."

He saw the hopeful gleam in her eyes. "You think so?"

Hell, he wasn't sure, but he'd never tell her that. "Yes, I think so."

She smiled. "Thanks, and I hope you're right."

He hoped he was right, too. They began walking again and when they reached the door to the room where Sunnie was being kept, he watched her square her shoulders and walk in. He followed behind her.

The baby was lying in a crib on her side, screaming up a storm, but miraculously, the moment she saw Sheila, her crying turned to tiny whimpers before she stopped completely. And Zeke wasn't sure how it was possible, but he wouldn't believe it if he hadn't seen it for himself.

The abandoned baby she'd named Sunnie smiled and reached her chubby arms out for her.

Four

The alarm went off and Zeke immediately came awake. Flipping over in bed, he stared up at the ceiling as his mind recalled everything that had happened the night before. Sunnie was now with Sheila.

He had hung around long enough to help gather up the baby and get her strapped in the car seat. And the kid hadn't uttered a single whimper. Instead, she had clung to Sheila like she was her very last friend on earth. He had followed them, just to make sure they arrived back at Sheila's house safely. While sitting in his truck, he had watched her get the baby inside before he'd finally pulled off.

At one point he'd almost killed the ignition and walked up to her door to see if she needed any more help, but figured he'd worn out his welcome already that day. Hell, at least he'd gotten a kiss out of the deal. And what a kiss he'd had. Thinking about that kiss had made it very difficult to fall asleep and kept him tossing and turning all night long.

His day would be full. Although Brad was his best friend, he was also a client; a client who'd come to him for help. Zeke wanted to solve this case quickly. Doing so would definitely be a feather in his cap. It would also further improve his reputation and boost the prospects of his new partner, Darius.

He eased out of bed and was about to slide his feet into his slippers, when the phone rang.

"Hello."

"Hi, Zeke. I just want to make sure the baby is okay."

He smiled at the sound of Darius's wife, Summer's, voice. Darius was presently in D.C. doing antiterrorism consulting work. "She's fine, Summer. The nurse who's going to be taking care of her for the next two weeks took her home from the hospital last night."

"What's the nurse's name?"

"Sheila Hopkins."

"I know Sheila."

He lifted a brow. "You do?"

"Yes… She and I worked together on a domestic-abuse case six months ago. The woman made it to the hospital while Sheila was working E.R. I was called in because the woman needed a place to stay."

Summer was the director of Helping Hands Women's Shelter in Somerset, their twin city. "I hope things turned out well for the woman," he said.

"It did, thanks to Sheila. She's a real professional."

He agreed. And he thought she was also a real woman. Before they'd gone to pick up the baby and while he was putting up the crib, she had showered and changed into a pair of jeans and a top. He wasn't aware that many curves could be on a woman's body. And he practically caught his breath each and every time he looked at her.

Moments later, after ending his call with Summer, Zeke drew in a deep breath and shook his head. He needed to focus on the case at hand and not the curvaceous Sheila Hopkins, or her sleep-stealing kisses.

The first thing he needed to do was to check the video cameras around the TCC. According to Brad, there were several, and Zeke was hoping that at least one of them had picked something up.

Then he intended to question the gardeners who were in charge of TCC's immaculate lawns to see if they'd seen or heard anything yesterday around the time the baby had been left on the doorstep.

And he had to meet up with Brad to make sure he'd taken the paternity test. The sooner they could prove that Brad wasn't Sunnie's father, the better.

As he made his way into the bathroom, he wondered how the baby was doing. Mainly he wondered how Sheila had fared. Last night, it had been evident after taking several naps that Sunnie was all bright-eyed and ready to play. At midnight. He wondered if Sheila got any sleep.

He rubbed his hands down his face. The thought of her in jammies beneath the covers had his gut stirring. Perhaps she didn't sleep under the covers. She might sleep on top of them the way he did sometimes. Then there was the possibility that she didn't wear jammies, but slept in the nude as he preferred doing at times, as well.

He could imagine her in the nude. For a moment he'd envisioned her that way last night when he'd heard the shower going and knew she was across the hall from where he was putting the crib together, and taking a shower and changing clothes. Strong desire had kicked him so hard he'd almost dropped his screwdriver.

And there was the scent he'd inhaled all through her house. It was a scent he now associated with her. Jasmine. He hadn't known what the aroma was until he'd asked. It was in her candles, various baskets of potpourri that she had scattered about. But he'd especially picked it up when she'd come out of her bedroom after taking her shower. She had evidently used the fragrance while showering because its scent shrouded her when she'd entered the room she would use as the temporary nursery.

Last night it had been hard to get to sleep. To take the chill out of the air he'd lit the fireplace in his bedroom and then couldn't settle down when visions of him and Sheila, naked in front of that same fireplace, tortured his mind.

As he brushed his teeth and washed his face, he couldn't help wondering what the hell was wrong with him. He knew the score where women were concerned. The feeling of being abandoned was something he would always deal with. As a result, he would never set himself up for that sort of pain again. No woman was worth it.

A short while later he had stepped out the shower and was drying off when his cell phone rang. He reached to pick it up off the bathroom counter and saw it was Brad. "What's going on?"

"Abigail Langley is what's going on. I know she has a meeting at TCC this morning and I'm going to have it out with her once and for all."

Zeke rolled his eyes. "Lay off her, Brad. You don't have any proof she's involved in any way."

"Sure she's involved. Abigail happens to be the only person who'll benefit if my reputation is ruined."

"But you just can't go accusing her of anything without concrete proof," Zeke said in a stern tone.

"I can't? Ha! Just watch me." Brad then clicked off the phone.

"Damn!" Zeke placed the phone back on the counter as he quickly began dressing. He needed to get over to TCC before Brad had a chance to confront Abigail Langley. He had a feeling his best friend was about to make a huge mistake.

Sheila fought back sleep as she fed Sunnie breakfast. She doubted if she and the baby had gotten a good four hours' sleep. The pediatric nurse had been right. Sunnie had slept most of yesterday, and in the middle of the night while most of Royal was sleeping, she had been wide awake and wanting to play.

Of course, Sheila had given in after numerous attempts at rocking her to sleep failed. Now Sunnie looked well-rested. Sheila refused to think about how *she* looked half asleep and yawning every ten minutes. But even lack of sleep could not erase how it felt holding the baby in her arms. And when Sunnie looked up at her and smiled, she knew she would willingly spend an entire week of sleepless nights to see that smile.

And she could make the cutest sounds when she was happy. It must be nice not having any troubles. Then she quickly remembered Sunnie might have troubles after all, if Bradford Price turned out not to be her daddy. Sheila didn't want to think about could happen to her once Social Services took her away and put her into the system.

"We're not going to think about any of that right now,

cupcake," she said, wiping Sunnie's mouth after she'd finished her bottle. "Now it's time for you to burp," she said, gently hoisting the baby onto her shoulder.

Dr. Phillips had referred Dr. Greene, the head pediatrician at Royal Memorial, to the case, and he had called inquiring how Sunnie was doing. He'd also given her helpful hints as to how to help Sunnie formulate a sleeping pattern where she would stay awake during most of the day and sleep longer at night.

A short while later, she placed the baby back in the crib after Sunnie seemed to have found interest in the mobile Zeke had purchased at the last minute while in the store last night. She had almost talked him out of getting it, but now she was glad she hadn't.

Sheila had pulled up a chair to sit there and watch Sunnie for a while, when her phone rang. She immediately picked it up. "Yes?"

"I was waiting to see if you remembered that you had a mother."

Sheila rolled her eyes, fighting the urge to say that she'd also been waiting to see if her mother remembered she had a daughter, but knew it would be a waste of time. The only reason her mother was calling her now was because she was in between husbands and she had a little idle time on her hands.

"Hi, Mom," she said, deciding not to bother addressing her mother's comment. "And how are you?"

"I could be better. Did you ever get that guy's phone number?"

That *guy* her mother was referring to was Dr. Morgan. The last time her mother had come to visit they had gone out to lunch, only to run into one of the surgeons from the hospital. Dr. Morgan was ten years her mother's junior.

Did that mean her mother was considering the possibility of becoming a cougar?

"No. Like I told you then, Dr. Morgan is already in a serious relationship."

Cassie Hopkins chuckled. "Isn't everybody...except you?"

Sheila cringed. Her mother couldn't resist the opportunity to dig. Cassie felt that if she could get five husbands, her only daughter should be able to get at least one. "I don't want a serious relationship, Mom."

"And if you did want one, then what?"

"Then I'd have one." Knowing her mother was about to jump in about Crawford Newman, the last man she wanted to talk about, she quickly changed the subject. "I talked to Lois the other day."

Her mother chuckled again. "And I bet you called her and not the other way around."

"No, in fact, she called me." She didn't have to tell her mother that Lois had called to tell her not to visit her and her family in Atlanta after all. And that was after issuing her an invitation earlier in the year. There was also no need to tell her that Lois had only issued the invitation after hearing about that heroic deed Sheila had performed, which had gotten broadcast nationwide on CNN. She guessed it wasn't important any longer for Lois to let anyone know that she was her sister after all.

Her mother snorted. "Hmmph. I'm surprised. So how is the princess doing and has she said when she plans to share any of the inheritance your father left her with you?"

Sheila knew the fact that her own father had intentionally left her out of his will still bothered her mother, although it no longer bothered her. It had at first because doing such a thing had pretty much proven what she'd always known. Her father hadn't wanted her. Regardless of the fact that he ended up despising her mother, that should not have had any bearing on his relationship with his daughter. But Baron Hopkins hadn't seen things that way. He saw her as an extension of her mother, and if you hated the mother then you automatically hated the child.

Lois, on the other hand, had indeed been her father's princess. The only child from the first wife whom he had adored, he hadn't been quite ready for the likes of Cassie. Things probably wouldn't have been so bad if Baron hadn't discovered her mother was having an affair with one of his business partners—a man who later became husband number two for Cassie. Then there was the question of whether Sheila was even his child, although she looked more like him than Lois did.

She was able to get her mother off the phone when Cassie had a call come through from some man. It was the story of her mother's life and the failed fairy tale for hers. She got out of the chair and moved over to the crib. Sunnie was trying to go to sleep. Sheila would have just loved to let her, but she knew if she were to sleep now that would mean another sleepless night.

"Oh, no you don't, sweetie pie," she said, getting the baby out of bed. "You and I are going to play for a while. I plan on keeping you up as much as possible today."

Sunnie gurgled and smiled sleepy hazel eyes up at her. "I know how you feel, trust me. I want to sleep, too. Hopefully, if this works, we'll both get to sleep tonight," Sheila said softy, rubbing the baby's fingers, reveling in just how soft her skin was.

Holding the baby gently in her arms, she headed downstairs.

* * *

Zeke walked down the hall of the TCC's clubhouse to one of the meeting rooms. The Texas Cattlemen's motto, which was clearly on display on a plaque in the main room here, said, Leadership, Justice and Peace. He heard loud angry voices and recognized Brad's and knew the female one belonged to Abigail. He wondered if they'd forgotten about the peace wording of the slogan.

"And just what are you accusing me of, Brad?"

"You're too intelligent to play dumb, Abigail. I know you're the one who arranged to have that baby left with a note claiming it's mine, when you know good and well it's not."

"What! How can you accuse me of such a thing?"

"Easily. You want to be the TCC's next president."

"And you think I'll go so far as to use a baby? A precious little baby to show you up?"

Zeke cringed. He could actually hear Abigail's voice breaking. Hell, it sounded as if the woman was crying. He paused outside the door.

"Dang, Abigail, I didn't mean to make you cry, for Pete's sake."

"Well, how could you accuse me of something like that? I love babies. And that little girl was abandoned. I had nothing to do with it, Brad. You've got to believe me."

Zeke inhaled deeply. The woman was downright bawling now. Brad had really gone and done it now.

"I'm sorry, Abby. I see that I was wrong. I didn't mean to get you so upset. I'm sorry."

"You should be. And to prove I'm not behind it," she said, still crying, "I suggest we suspend campaigning for the election until the case is solved."

"And you'll go along with doing that?"

"Of course. We're talking about a baby, Brad, and her welfare comes first."

"I agree," Brad said. *"Thanks, Abby. And again I'm sorry for accusing you earlier."*

Zeke thought it was time for him to make his entrance before Brad made a bigger mess of things. At least he'd had the sense to apologize to the woman. He opened the door and stopped. Brad was standing in the middle of the room holding a still-weeping Abigail in his arms.

For a moment Zeke thought he should tiptoe back out and was about to do just that, when they both glanced over at him. And as if embarrassed at being caught in such an embrace, the two quickly jumped part.

Zeke placed his hands in the pockets of his jeans and smiled at the pair. "Brad. Abigail. Does this mean the two of you are no longer at war?"

A short while later Zeke was getting back in his car thinking that he hadn't needed to put out the fire after all. Brad and Abigail were a long way from being best friends, but at least it seemed as if they'd initiated a truce. If he hadn't been a victim of abandonment himself, he would think something good had at least resulted from Sunnie's appearance.

Sunnie.

He shook his head. Sheila had deemed the baby be called Sunnie for the time being, and everyone had pretty much fallen in line with her request. He had refrained from calling her earlier just in case she and the baby were sleeping in late. But now it was close to two in the afternoon. Surely they were up by now. While she had been upstairs taking a shower last night, he had opened her refrigerator to grab another beer and noticed hers was barer than his. That meant, also like him, she must eat out a lot. Chances were she wouldn't want to take the baby out, so the least he could do would be to be a good guy and stop somewhere, buy something for her to eat and take it to her.

While at the TCC he had checked and nothing had gotten caught on the video camera other than a woman's hand placing the baby on the doorstep. Whoever had done it seemed to have known just where the cameras were located, which meant the culprit was someone familiar with the grounds of the club. Could it have been an inside job? At least they knew they could erase Abigail off the list. She had been in a meeting when the baby had been dropped off.

Besides, to say Abigail Langley had gotten emotional as a result of Brad's accusation was an understatement. He couldn't help wondering why. He knew she was a widow. Had she lost a baby at some point while she'd been married? He'd been tempted to ask Brad but figured knowing his and Abigail's history, he would probably be the last to know. He'd heard from more than one source that the two of them had been butting heads since they were kids.

After buckling his seat belt he turned his car's ignition and eased out the parking lot, wondering what type of meal Sheila might have a taste for. Still not wanting to disturb her and the baby, he smiled, thinking, when in doubt, get pizza.

Sheila cocked one eye open as she gazed over at Sunnie, who was back in the crib toying with her mobile again. She sighed, not sure how long she would be able to stay awake. It had been almost eighteen hours now.

She'd done doubles at the hospital before, but at least she'd gotten a power nap in between. She didn't know babies had so much energy. She thought of closing her eyes for a second, but figured there was no way for her to do something like that. Mothers didn't sleep while their babies were awake, did they?

She had tried everything and refused to drink another cup of coffee. The only good thing was that if she continued to keep Sunnie awake, that meant when they both went to sleep, hopefully, it would be through the night. She glanced around the room, liking how it looked and hoped Sunnie liked it as well.

Zeke had been such a sweetheart to help her put the baby equipment together and hang pictures on the wall. Although he hadn't asked, he had to have been wondering why she was going overboard for a baby that would be in her care for only two weeks. She was glad he hadn't asked because she would not have known what to tell him.

She tried to ignore the growling of her stomach and the fact that other than toast, coffee and an apple, she hadn't eaten anything else that day. She didn't want to take her eyes off the baby for even a minute.

She nearly jumped when she heard the sound of the doorbell. She glanced at the Big Bird clock she'd hung on the wall. It was close to four in the afternoon. She moved over to the window and glanced down and saw the two-seater sports car in her driveway and knew who it belonged to. What was Zeke doing back? They had exchanged numbers last night, merely as a courtesy. She really hadn't expected to see him again any time soon.

She immediately thought about the kiss they'd shared...not that she hadn't thought about it several times that day already. That was the kind of kiss a girl would want to tell somebody about. Like a girlfriend. She'd thought about calling Jill then had changed her mind. On second thought, maybe it was the kind of kiss a girl should keep to herself.

The doorbell sounded again. Knowing she probably looked a mess and, at the moment, not caring since she hadn't anticipated any visitors, she walked over to the bed and picked up the baby. "Come on, Sunnie. Looks like we have company."

Zeke was just about to turn to leave, when the door opened. All it took was one look at Sheila to know she'd had a rough night and an even rougher day. Sunnie, on the other hand, looked happy and well-rested.

"Hey, you okay?" he asked Sheila when she stepped aside to let him in. And he figured the only reason she'd done that was because of the pizza boxes he was carrying.

"I'm fine." She eyed the pizza box. "And I hope you brought that to share. I've barely eaten all day."

"Yes, I brought it to share," he said, heading for the kitchen. "The kid wore you out today?"

"And last night," she said, following on his heels. "I talked to the pediatrician about her not sleeping through the night and he suggested I try to keep her awake today. That means staying awake myself."

He stopped and she almost walked into the back of him. He turned inquisitive dark eyes on her. "Sunnie hasn't taken a nap at all today?"

"No. Like I said, I'm keeping her awake so we can both sleep tonight."

He found that interesting for some reason. "When do babies usually develop a better sleep pattern?"

"It depends. Usually they would have by now. But we

don't know Sunnie's history. Her life might have been so unstable she hadn't gotten adjusted to anything." She glanced at the baby. "I hate talking about her like she isn't here."

Zeke laughed. "It's not as if she can understand anything you've said."

He shook his head. Sheila had to be pretty tired to even concern herself with anything like that. He glanced around the kitchen. It was still neat as a pin, but baby bottles lined the counter as well as a number of other baby items. It was obvious that a baby was in residence.

"Why did you stop by?" she asked.

He glanced back at her. Her eyes looked tired, almost dead on her feet. Her hair was tied back in a ponytail and she wasn't wearing any makeup. But he thought she looked good. "To check on the two of you. And I figured you probably hadn't had a chance to cook anything," he said, deciding not to mention he'd noticed last night she hadn't had anything to cook.

"So I decided I would be nice and stop and grab something for you," he said, placing the pizza boxes on the table. He opened one of them.

"Oh, that smells so good. Thank you."

He chuckled. "I've gotten pizza from this place before and it is good. And you're welcome. Do you want to lay her down while you dig in?"

She looked down at Sunnie and then back at him. "Lay her down?"

"Yes, like in that crib I put together for her last night."

"But…she'll be all alone."

He frowned. "Yes, but I hooked up that baby monitor last night so you could hear her. Haven't you tried it out?"

"Yes, but I like watching her."

He nodded slowly. "Why? I can imagine you being fascinated by her since you admitted yesterday that you've never kept a baby before, but why the obsession? You're a nurse. Haven't you worked in the nursery before?"

"Of course, but this is different. This is my home and Sunnie is in my care. I don't want anything to happen to her."

He could tell by her tone that she was getting a little defensive, so he decided to back off a bit, table it for later. And there would definitely be a later, because she wouldn't be much use to Sunnie or anybody if she wore herself out. "Fine, sit down and I'll go get that extra car seat. You can place her in it while you eat."

A short while later they were sitting at her kitchen table with Sunnie sitting in the car seat on the floor between them. She was moving her hands to and fro while making sounds. She seemed like such a happy baby. Totally different from the baby that had been screaming up a storm yesterday. Every once in a while she would raise her hazel eyes to stare at them. Mainly at him. It was as if she was trying to figure him out. Determine if he was safe.

Zeke glanced over at Sheila. She had eaten a couple slices of pizza along with the bag salad he'd bought. Every so often she would yawn, apologize and then yawn again. She needed to get some sleep; otherwise, she would fall on her face at any minute.

"Thanks for the pizza, Zeke. Not only are you nice, but you're thoughtful."

He leaned back in his chair. "You're welcome." He paused for a moment. "I got a folder with stuff out there in my car that I need to go over. I can do it here just as well as anywhere else."

Her forehead furrowed as if confused. "But why would you want to?"

He smiled. "That way I can watch Sunnie."

She still looked confused.

"Look, Sheila. It's obvious that you're tired. Probably ready to pass out. You can go upstairs and take a nap while I keep an eye on the baby."

"But why would you want to do something like that?"

He chuckled. She asked a lot of questions. Unfortunately for him they were questions he truly couldn't answer. Why had he made such an offer? He really wasn't sure. All he knew was that he liked being around her and wasn't ready to leave yet.

When he didn't give her an answer quick enough, she narrowed her gaze. "You think I can't handle things, don't you? You think I've taken on more than I can chew by agreeing to be Sunnie's temporary foster parent. You think—"

Before she could finish her next words, he was out of the chair, had eased around the baby and had pulled Sheila into his arms. "Right now I think you're talking too damn much." And then he kissed her.

For some reason he needed to do this, he thought as his mouth took possession of hers. And the instant their mouths touched, he felt energized in a way he'd never felt before. Sexually energized. His tongue slid between her parted lips and immediately began tangling with hers. What was there about kissing her that was so mind-blowing, so arousing, so threatening to his senses?

This kind of mouth interaction with her was stirring things inside him he'd tried to keep at bay with other women. How could she rouse them so effortlessly? So deeply and so thoroughly? And why did she feel so damn good in his arms? Even better today than yesterday.

Yesterday there had been that element of surprise on both their parts. It was still there today, but surprise was being smothered by heat of the most erotic kind.

And it was heat he could barely handle. Not sure that he could manage. But it was heat that he was definitely enjoying. And then there was something else trying to creep into the mix. Emotions. Emotions he wasn't accustomed to. He had thought of her all day. Why? Usually for him it had always been out of sight and out of mind. But not with Sheila. The woman was unforgettable. She was temptation he couldn't resist.

He felt a touch on his leg and reluctantly released Sheila's mouth to glance down. Hazel eyes were staring up at him. Sunnie had grabbed hold of his pant leg. He couldn't help chuckling. At five months old the kid was seeing too much. If she hadn't gotten his attention, he'd probably still be kissing Sheila.

He shifted his gaze from the baby back to the woman he was still holding in his arms. She was about to step back, so he tightened his hold around her waist. "I'm going out to my car and get my briefcase. When I come back inside you're going to go up those stairs and get some rest. I'll handle Sunnie."

"But—"

"No buts. No questions. I'll take good care of her. I promise."

"She might cry the entire time"

"If she cries I'll deal with it." He then walked out of the kitchen.

Sheila couldn't stop her smile when Zeke walked out. She glanced down at Sunnie. "He's kind of bossy, isn't he?" She touched her lips. "And he's a darn good kisser."

She sighed deeply. "Not that you needed to know that. Not that you needed to see us lock lips, either."

She then moved around the kitchen as she cleared off the table. She was standing at the sink when Zeke returned with his briefcase. "How long do you plan to be here?" she asked him.

"For as long as you need to rest."

She nodded. "I'll be fine in a couple of hours. Will you wake me?"

Zeke stared at her, fully aware she had no idea of what she was asking of him. Seeing her in bed, under the covers or on top of the covers, would not be a good idea. At least she hadn't reminded him that she'd told him not to kiss her again. But what could she say, when she had kissed him back?

"I won't wake you, Sheila. You have to wake up on your own."

She frowned. "But Sunnie will need a bath later."

"And she'll get one, with or without you. For your information I do know a little about kids."

She looked surprised. "You do?"

"Yes. I was raised by my aunt and she has a daughter with twins. They consider me their uncle and I've kept them before."

"Both?"

"Yes, and at the same time. It was a piece of cake." Okay, he had exaggerated some. There was no need to tell her that they had almost totally wrecked his place by the time their parents had returned.

"How old are they?"

"Now they're four. The first time I kept them they were barely one."

She nodded. "They live in Austin?"

"No. New Orleans."

"So you're not a Texan by birth?"

He wondered why all the questions again. He had made a mistake when he mentioned Alicia and the twins. "According to my birth certificate, I am a Texan by birth. My aunt who raised me lives in New Orleans. I returned to Texas when I attended UT in Austin."

He had told her enough and, when she opened her mouth to say something more, he placed his hand over it. Better his hand than his mouth. "No more questions. Now, off to bed."

She glanced down at the baby when he removed his hand from her mouth. "Are you sure you want to handle her?"

"Positive. Now, go."

She hesitated for a minute and then drew in a deep breath before leaving the kitchen. He glanced down at Sunnie, whose eyes had followed Sheila from the room. Then those same hazel eyes latched on to him almost in an accusatory stare. Her lips began trembling and he had an idea what was coming next. When she let out a wail, he bent down and picked up the car seat and set it on the table.

"Shh, little one. Sheila needs her rest. Come on, I'm not that bad. She likes me. I kissed her. Get over it."

When her crying suddenly slowed to a low whimper, he wondered if perhaps this kid did understand.

Five

Something—Sheila wasn't sure exactly what—woke her up, and her gaze immediately went to the clock on the nightstand: 7:00 p.m. She quickly slid out of bed and raced down the stairs then halted at the last step. There, stretched out on the sofa was Zeke with Sunnie on his chest. They were both asleep and, since the baby was wearing one of the cute pj sets they'd purchased yesterday, it was obvious he'd given her a bath. In fact, the air was filled with the fragrance of baby oil mixed with baby powder. She liked the smell.

She wished she had a camera to take a picture. This was definitely a Kodak moment. She slowly tiptoed to the chair across from the sofa and sat down. Even while sleeping, Zeke was handsome, and his long lashes almost fanned his upper cheeks. He didn't snore. Crawford snored something awful. Another comparison of the two men.

She wondered if he'd ever dumped a woman the

way Crawford had dumped her. Good old Crawford, the traveling salesman, who spent a lot of time on the road…and as she later found out while he'd been on the road, in other women's beds. She remembered the time she would anxiously await his long-distance calls and how she would feel when she didn't get them. How lonely she would be when she didn't hear from him for days.

And she would never forget that day when he did show back up, just to let her know he was marrying someone else. A woman he'd met while out peddling his medical supplies. He had wanted her to get on with her life because he had gotten on with his. She took his advice. Needing to leave Dallas, the next time an opportunity came for a transfer to another hospital, she had taken it.

She continued to stare at Zeke and wondered what his story was. He'd told her bits and pieces and she figured that was all she would get. So far he hadn't mentioned anything about a mother. His comment yesterday pretty much sealed the fact he hadn't known his father. And from what he'd told her today, his aunt in New Orleans had raised him. Had his mother died? She drew in a deep breath, thinking it really wasn't any of her business. Still, she couldn't help being curious about the hunk stretched out on her sofa. The man who had kissed her twice. The man who'd literally knocked sense right out of her brain.

And that wasn't good. That meant it was time for him to leave. Yesterday she had appreciated his help in shopping with her for baby items. Today she appreciated the pizza. There couldn't be a tomorrow.

Easing out of the chair, she crossed the room and gently shook him awake. She sucked in a deep breath when his eyes snapped open and his beautiful dark eyes stared up at her. Pinned her to the spot where she was standing. They didn't say anything but stared at each other for the longest time. She felt his stare as if his gaze was a physical caress.

And while he stared at her, she remembered things. She remembered how good his mouth felt on hers. How delicious his tongue tasted in her mouth. How his tongue would slide from side to side while driving her to the brink of madness. It made her wonder just what else that tongue was capable of doing.

She blushed and she knew he'd noticed because his gaze darkened. "What were you thinking just now?"

Did he really expect her to tell him? Fat chance! Some things he was better off not knowing and that was definitely one of them. "I was thinking that it's time for me to put Sunnie to bed."

"I doubt that would have made you blush."

She doubted it, too, but she would never admit to it. Instead of responding to what he'd said, she reached for Sunnie. "I'm taking her upstairs and putting her to bed." Once she had the baby cradled in her arms, she walked off.

When she had gone up the stairs, Zeke eased into a sitting position and rubbed his hands down his face. Surprisingly, he'd gotten a lot of work done. Sunnie had sat in her car seat and stared at him the entire time, evidently fascinated by the shifting of the papers and the sight of him working on his laptop computer. He figured the bright colors that had occasionally flashed across the screen had fascinated her.

He stood and went back into the kitchen. There was no doubt in his mind that when Sheila returned she would expect him to be packed up and ready to go. He

would not disappoint her. Although he would love to
hang around, he needed to haul it. There was too much
attraction between them. Way too much chemistry.
When they had gazed into each other's eyes, the air
had become charged. She had become breathless. So
had he. That wasn't good.

All there was supposed to be between them was
business. Where was his hard-and-fast rule never to mix
business with pleasure? It had taken a hard nosedive the
first time he'd kissed her. And if that hadn't been bad
enough, he'd kissed her again. What had come over
him? He knew the answer without thinking—lust of
the most intense kind.

By the time he clicked his briefcase closed, he heard
Sheila come back downstairs, and when she walked
into the kitchen he had it in his hand. "Walk me to the
door," he said softly, wondering why he'd asked her to
do so when he knew the way out.

"Okay."

She silently walked beside him and when they got
to the door, she reached out to open it, but he took her
hand, brought it to his lips and kissed it. "I left my card
on the table. Call me if you need anything. Otherwise,
this was my last time coming by."

She nodded and didn't ask why. He knew she understood. They were deeply attracted to each other and if they
hung around each other for long, that attraction would heat
up and lead to something else. Something that he knew
neither of them wanted to tangle with right now.

"Thanks for everything, Zeke. I feel rested."

He smiled. "But you can always use more. She'll
probably sleep through the night, but she'll be active in
the morning. That little girl has a lot of energy."

Sheila chuckled. "So you noticed."

"Oh, yeah, I noticed. But she's a good kid."

"Yes, and I still can't believe someone abandoned her."

"It happens, Sheila. Even to good kids."

He brushed a kiss across her lips. "Go back to bed." Then he opened the door and walked out.

Zeke forced himself to keep moving and not look back. He opened the car door and sat there a moment, fighting the temptation to get out of his car, walk right back up to her door and knock on it. When she answered it, he would kiss her senseless before she could say a single word. He would then sweep her off her feet and take her up to her bedroom and stretch her out on it, undress her and then make love to her.

He leaned back against the headrest and closed his eyes. How had it moved from kissing to thoughts of making love to her? *Easily, Travers,* his mind screamed. She's a beauty. She's hot. And you enjoy her mouth too damn much.

He took a deep breath and then exhaled slowly. He would be doing the right thing by staying away. Besides, it wasn't as though he didn't have anything to do. He had several people to interview tomorrow, including several TCC members who wanted to talk to him. One of them had called tonight requesting the meeting and he wondered what it would be about.

He turned the key in the ignition and backed out the driveway. He looked at the house one last time before doing so. All the lights were off downstairs. His gaze traveled to her bedroom window. The light was on there. He wondered what she was doing. Probably getting ready for bed.

A bed he wished he could join her in.

* * *

Sheila checked on Sunnie one more time before going into her bathroom to take a shower. She felt heat rush to her cheeks when she remembered waking Zeke earlier. The man had a way of looking at her that could turn her bones into mush.

A short while later after taking a shower and toweling dry her body, she slid into a pair of pajamas. She checked on Sunnie one last time and also made sure the monitor was set so she could hear her if she was to awaken. Zeke was convinced the baby would sleep through the night.

She drew in a deep breath knowing he'd told her he wouldn't be back. And she knew it was for the best. She would miss him. His appearance at her door tonight had been a surprise. But he had a way of making himself useful and she liked that. Crawford hadn't been handy with tools. He used to tell her he worked too hard to do anything other than what was required of him at his job. Not even taking out the trash.

And she had put up with it because she hadn't wanted to be alone.

Moving here was her first accomplishment. It had been a city where she hadn't known anybody. A city where she would be alone. Go figure. She had gotten used to it and now Zeke had invaded her space. So had Sunnie. The latter was a welcome invasion; the former wasn't.

As she slid into bed and drew the covers around her, she closed her eyes and ran her tongue around her mouth. Even after brushing her teeth she could still taste Zeke. It was as if his flavor was embedded in her mouth. She liked it. She would savor it because it wouldn't happen again.

* * *

The next day, Zeke leaned back on the table and studied the two men sitting before him and tried digesting their admissions.

"So the two of you are saying that you also received blackmail letters?"

Rali Tariq and Arthur Moran, well-known wealthy businessmen and longtime members of the TCC, nodded. Then Rali spoke up. "Although I was innocent of what the person was accusing me of, I was afraid to go to the authorities."

"Same here," Arthur said. "I was hoping the person would eventually go away when I didn't acknowledge the letters. It was only when I found out about the blackmailing scheme concerning Bradford that I figured I needed to come forward."

"That's the reason I'm here, as well," Rali added.

Zeke nodded. What the two men had just shared with him certainly brought a lot to light. It meant the blackmailer hadn't just targeted Brad, but had set his or her mark on other innocent, unsuspecting TCC members, as well. That made him wonder whether the individual was targeting TCC members because they were known to be wealthy or if there was a personal vendetta the authorities needed to be concerned with.

"Did you bring the letters with you?"

"Yes."

Both men handed him their letters. He placed them on the table and then pulled out one of the ones Brad had received. It was obvious they had been written by the same person.

"They looked the same," Rali said, looking over Zeke's shoulder at all three letters.

Arthur nodded in agreement.

"Yes, it appears that one person wrote them all," Zeke replied. "But the question is why did he carry out his threat against Brad but not on you two?"

He could tell by the men's expressions that they didn't have a clue. "Well, at least I'm finally getting pieces to the puzzle. I appreciate the two of you coming forward. It will help in clearing Brad's name. Now all we have to do is wait for the results of the paternity test."

An hour later he met Brad for lunch at Claire's Restaurant, an upscale establishment in downtown Royal that served delicious food. A smile curved Brad's lips after hearing about Zeke's meeting with Rali and Arthur.

"Then that should settle things," he said, cutting into the steak on his plate. "If Rali and Arthur received blackmail letters, that proves there's a conspiracy against members of the TCC. There probably are others who aren't coming forward like Rali and Arthur."

Zeke took a sip of his wine. "Possibly. But you are the only one who he or she carried out the threat with. Why you and not one of the others? Hell, Rali is the son of a sheikh. I would think they would have stuck it to him real good. So we still aren't out of the woods. There's something about the whole setup that bothers me."

He studied Brad for a moment. "Did you and Abigail Langley clear things up?"

Brad met his gaze. "If you're asking if I think she's still involved then the answer is no. Now I wished I hadn't approached her with my accusations."

A smile touched Zeke's lips. "I hate to say I told you so, but I did tell you so."

"I know. I know. But Abigail and I have been bad news for years."

"Yeah, but someone getting on your bad side is one thing, Brad. Accusing someone, especially a woman, of having anything to do with abandoning a child is another."

Brad held his gaze for the longest time. "And you of all people should know, right?"

Zeke nodded. "Yes, I should know."

Zeke took another sip of his wine. As his best friend, Brad was one of the few people who knew his history. Brad knew how Zeke's mother had abandoned him. Not on a doorstep, but in the care of his aunt. Although his aunt had been a godsend, he'd felt abandoned those early years. Alone. Discarded. Thrown away. No longer wanted.

It had taken years for him to get beyond those childhood feelings. But he would be the first to admit those childhood feelings had subsequently become adult hang-ups. That was one of the reasons he only engaged in casual affairs. He wouldn't let anyone walk out on him again. He would be the one doing the walking.

"Abigail certainly took my accusation hard," Brad said, breaking into Zeke's thoughts. "I've known her since we were kids and I've never known her to be anything but tough as nails. Seeing her break down like that really got to me."

"I could tell. You seemed to be holding her pretty tightly when I walked in."

He chuckled at the blush that appeared in Brad's features. "Well, what else was I supposed to do?" Brad asked. "Especially since I was the reason she'd gotten upset in the first place. I'm going to have to watch what I say around her."

Especially if it's about babies, Zeke thought, deciding not to say the words out loud. If Brad wasn't concerned with the reason the woman fell to pieces then he wouldn't be concerned with it, either. Besides, he had enough on his plate.

"So how's the baby?" Brad asked, breaking into his thoughts yet again.

"Sunnie?"

"Yes."

He leaned back in his chair as he thought about how she had wet him up pretty good when he'd given her a bath. He'd had to throw his shirt into Sheila's dryer. "She's fine. I checked on her yesterday."

"And the woman that's taking care of her. That nurse. She's doing a pretty good job?"

Zeke thought about Sheila. Hell, he'd thought about her a lot today, whether he had wanted to or not. "Yes, she's doing a pretty good job."

"Well, I hope the results from the paternity test come up quickly enough for her sake."

Zeke lifted a brow. "Why for her sake?"

"I would hate for your nurse to get too attached to the baby."

Zeke nodded. He would hate for "his" nurse to get too attached to Sunnie, as well.

"She is such a cutie," Summer Franklin said as she held Sunnie in her arms. Surprisingly, Sunnie hadn't cried when Summer had taken her out of Sheila's arms. She was too fascinated with Summer's dangling earrings to care.

Sheila liked Summer. She was one of the few people she felt she could let her guard down around. Because Sheila had a tendency to work all the time, this was the first time she'd seen Summer in weeks.

"Yes, she is a cutie," Sheila said. "I can't imagine anyone abandoning her like that."

"Me, neither. But you better believe Zeke's going to get to the bottom of it. I'm glad Darius brought him on as a partner. My husband was working himself to death solving cases. Now he has help."

Sheila nodded, wondering how much Summer knew about Zeke, but didn't want to ask for fear her friend would wonder why.

Although Sunnie had slept through the night, she herself, on the other hand, had not. Every time she closed her eyes she had seen Zeke, looking tall, dark, handsome and fine as any man had a right to be. Then she also saw another image of him. The one sleeping peacefully on the sofa with the baby lying on his chest. She wondered if he would marry and have children one day. She had a feeling he would make a great dad just from his interaction with Sunnie.

"Oops, I think she's ready to return to you now," Summer said, breaking her thoughts. She smiled when she saw Sunnie lift her little hands to reach out for her, making her feel special. Wanted. Needed.

"You're good with her, Sheila."

She glanced over at Summer and smiled. "Thanks."

"I wonder who her real parents are."

"I wondered that as well. But I'm sure Zeke is going to find out," Sheila said.

Summer chuckled. "I believe that, as well. Zeke comes across as a man who's good at what he does."

Sheila held the baby up to hide the blush on her face. She knew for a fact that Zeke was good at what he did, especially when it came to kissing a woman.

Zeke let himself inside his home with a bunch of papers in his hand, closing the door behind him with the heel of his shoe. He'd been busy today.

He dropped the papers on his dining room table and headed straight to the kitchen to grab a beer out of the refrigerator. He took a huge gulp and then let out a deep breath. He'd needed that. That satisfied his thirst. Now if he could satisfy his hunger for Sheila Hopkins the same way...

Twice he had thought of dropping by her place and twice he had remembered why he could not do that. He had no reason to see her again until it was time to open the paternity test results. Considering what he'd discovered with those other two TCC members, he felt confident that the test would prove there was no biological link between Brad and Sunnie. But he was just as determined to discover whose baby she was. What person would abandon their child to make them a part of some extortion scheme? It was crazy. And sick. And he intended to determine who would do such a thing and make sure the authorities threw the book at them as hard as they could.

His thoughts shifted back to Sheila as he moved from the kitchen to the dining room. He had a lot of work to do and intended to get down to business. But he couldn't get out of his mind how he had opened his eyes while stretched out on her sofa only to find her staring down at him. If he hadn't had the baby sleeping on his chest, he would have been tempted to reach out and pull her down on the sofa with him. And he would have taken her mouth the way he wanted to do. Why was he torturing himself by thinking of something he was better off not having?

He drew in a deep breath, knowing he needed to put Sheila out of his mind. He had been going through various reports when the phone rang. He grinned when he saw it was Darius.

"Homesick, Darius?" he asked into the phone, and heard a resounding chuckle.

"Of course. I'm not missing you though. It's my wife. I'm trying to talk Summer into catching a plane and joining me here—especially since there's a hurricane too close to you guys for comfort, but they're shorthanded at the shelter."

"So I heard."

"She also told me about the abandoned baby. How's that going?"

He took the next few minutes to bring Darius up to date. "I know Bradford Price and if he says the baby isn't his then it's not his," Darius said. "He has no reason to lie about it."

"I know, that's why I intend to expose the jerk who's out to ruin Brad's good name," Zeke said.

Six

Three days later Sheila sat glued to her television listening to the weather report. It was the last month of hurricane season and wouldn't you know it…Hurricane Spencer was up to no good out in the gulf. Forecasters were advising everyone to take necessary precautions by stocking up on the essentials just in case the storm changed course. Now Sheila had Sunnie to worry about, and that meant making sure she had enough of everything—especially disposable diapers, formula and purified water in case the power went out.

Sunnie had pretty much settled down and was sleeping through the night. And they were both getting into a great routine. During the day Sheila had fun entertaining the baby by taking her to the park and other kid-friendly places. She enjoyed pushing Sunnie around in the stroller. Sunnie would still cry on occasion when others held her, but once she would glance around and lock her gaze on Sheila, she was fine.

Sheila had put the baby to bed a short while ago and was ready to go herself if only she was sleepy. Over the past couple of days she'd had several visitors. In addition to Summer and Jill, Dr. Greene had stopped by to check on the baby and Ms. Talbert from Social Services had visited, as well. Ms. Talbert had praised her for volunteering to care for Sunnie and indicated that considering the baby was both healthy and happy, she was doing a great job. The woman had further indicated there was a possibility the results of the paternity test might come in earlier than the two weeks anticipated. Instead of jumping for joy at the news, Sheila had found herself hoping that would not be the case. She had been looking forward to her two weeks with Sunnie.

She heard a branch hit the window and jumped. It had been windy all day and now it seemed it was getting windier. Forecasters predicted the hurricane would make landfall sometime after midnight. They predicted that Royal would be spared the worst of it.

She glanced around the room where she had already set out candles. The lights had been blinking all day; she hoped she didn't lose power, but had to be prepared if she did.

She was halfway up the stairs when the house suddenly went black.

The winds have increased and we have reports of power outages in certain sections of Royal, including the Meadowland and LeBaron areas. Officials are working hard to restore power to these homes and hope to do so within the next few hours…

Zeke was stretched out on the sofa with his eyes

closed, but the announcement that had just blared from the television made him snap them open. He then slid into a sitting position. Sheila lived in the Meadowland area.

He knew he had no reason to be concerned. Hopefully, like everyone else, she had anticipated the possibility of a power failure and was prepared. But what if she wasn't? What if she was across town sitting on her sofa holding the baby in the dark?

Standing, he rubbed a hand down his face. It had been four days since he'd seen or talked to her. Four days, while working on clearing Brad's name, of trying hard to push thoughts of her to the back of his mind. He'd failed often, when no matter what he was working on, his thoughts drifted back to her.

What was there about a woman when a man couldn't get her out of his mind? When he would think of her during his every waking moment and wake up in the middle of the night with thoughts of her when he should be sleeping?

Zeke stretched his body before grabbing his keys off the table. Pushing aside the thought that he was making a mistake by rushing off to check on the very woman he'd sworn to stay away from, he quickly walked toward the door, grabbing a jacket and his Stetson on the way out.

Sheila glanced around the living room. Candles were lit and flashlights strategically placed where she might need them. It was just a little after ten but the wind was still howling outside. When she had looked out the window moments ago, all she could do was stare into darkness. Everything was total black.

She had checked on Sunnie earlier and the baby was

sleeping peacefully, oblivious to what was happening, and that was good. Sunnie had somehow kicked the covers off her pudgy little legs and Sheila had recovered her, gazing down at her while thinking what the future held for such a beautiful little girl.

Sheila left the nursery and walked downstairs. She had the radio on a station that played jazz while occasionally providing updates on the storm. It had stopped raining, but the sound of water dripping off the roof was stirring a feeling inside her that she was all too familiar with—loneliness.

Deciding what she needed was a glass a wine, she was headed to the kitchen when she heard the sound of her cell phone. She quickly picked it up and from caller ID saw it was Zeke.

She felt the thud in her chest at the same time she felt her pulse rate increase. "Yes?"

"I'm at the door."

Taking a deep breath and trying to keep her composure intact, she headed toward the door. The police had asked for cars not to be on the road unless it was absolutely necessary due to dangerous conditions, so why was he here? Did he think she couldn't handle things during a power failure? She was certain Sunnie was his main concern and not her.

She opened the door and her breath caught. He stood there looking both rugged and handsome, dressed in a tan rawhide jacket, Western shirt and jeans and a Stetson on his head. The reflections from the candles played across his features as he gazed at her. "I heard the reports on television. Are you and the baby okay?"

She nodded, at the moment unable to speak. Swallowing deeply, she finally said, "Yes, we're fine."

"That's good. May I come in?"

Their gazes stayed locked and she knew what her response should be. They had agreed there was no reason for him to visit her and Sunnie. But the only thing she could think about at that moment was the loneliness that had been seeping through her body for the past few hours, and that she hadn't seen him in four days. And whether she wanted to admit it or not, she had missed him.

"Please come in." She stepped aside.

Removing his hat, Zeke walked past Sheila and glanced around. Lit candles were practically everywhere, and the scent of jasmine welcomed his nostrils. A blaze was also roaring in the fireplace, which radiated a warm, cozy atmosphere.

"Do you want me to take your jacket?"

He glanced back at her. "Yes. Thanks."

He removed his jacket and handed it to her, along with his hat. He watched as she placed both on the coatrack. She was wearing a pair of gold satin pajamas that looked cute on her.

"I was about to have a glass of wine," she said. "Do you want to join me?"

He could say that he'd only come to check on her and the baby, and because they seem to be okay, he would be going. That might have worked if he hadn't asked to come in…or he hadn't taken off his jacket. "Yes, I'd love to have a glass. Thanks."

"I'll be back in a minute."

He watched her leave and slowly moved toward the fireplace. She seemed to be taking his being there well. A part of him was surprised, considering their agreement, that she hadn't asked him to leave. He was glad she hadn't. He watch the fire blazing in the fireplace while thinking that he hadn't realized just how much he had missed seeing her until she'd opened the door. She looked so damn good and it had taken everything within him not to pull her into his arms and kiss her, the way he'd done those other two times. Hell, he was counting, mainly because there was no way he could ever forget them.

And as he stood there and continued to gaze into the fire, he thought of all the reasons he should grab his jacket and hat and leave before she returned. For starters, he wanted her, which was a good enough reason in itself. And the degree to which he wanted her would be alarming to most. But he had wanted her from the beginning. He had walked into the hospital and seen her standing there holding the baby, and looking like the beautiful woman that she was. He had been stunned at the intensity of the desire that had slammed into him; it had almost toppled him. But he had been able to control it by concentrating on the baby, making Sunnie's care his top priority.

However, he hadn't been able to control himself that day at his place when she had gotten in his face. Nor had he been able to handle things the last time he was here and he'd nearly mauled her mouth off. Being around her was way too risky.

Then why was he here? And why was his heart thumping deep in his chest anticipating her return? At that moment he had little control of what he was feeling; especially because they were emotions he hadn't ever felt before for a woman. If it was just a sexual thing he would be able to handle that. But the problem was that he wasn't sure it was. He definitely wanted her, but there was something about her he didn't understand. There were reasons he couldn't fathom as to why he was so attracted to her. And there was no way he could use

Sunnie as an excuse. Sunnie might be the reason they had initially met, but the baby had nothing to do with him being here now and going through the emotions he was feeling.

"Do you think this bad weather will last long?"

He turned around to face her and wished he hadn't. She had two glasses in her hand and a bottle of wine under her arm. But what really caught his attention was the way the firelight danced across her features, combined with the glow from the candles. She looked like a woman he wanted to make love to. Damn.

She was temptation.

Zeke moved to assist her with the glasses and wine bottle, and the moment their hands touched, he was a goner. Taking both glasses, as well as the wine bottle, from her hands, he placed both on the table. And then he turned back to her, drew her into his arms and lowered his mouth to hers.

Sheila went into his arms willingly, their bodies fusing like metal to magnet. She intended to go with the flow. And boy was she rolling. All over the place.

She could feel his hand in the small of her back that gently pressed her body even closer to his. And she felt him. At the juncture of her thighs. His erection was definitely making its presence known by throbbing hard against her. It was kicking her desire into overdrive. And she could definitely say that was something that had never happened to her before. Since her breakup with Crawford she had kept to herself. Hadn't wanted to date anyone. Preferred not getting involved with any living male.

But being in Zeke's arms felt absolutely perfect. And the way he was mating his mouth with hers was stirring a yearning within her she hadn't been aware she was capable of feeling. And when he finally released her mouth, he let her know he wasn't through with her when his teeth grazed the skin right underneath her right ear, causing shivers to flow through her. And then his teeth moved lower to her collarbone and began sucking gently there.

She tilted her head back and groaned deeply in her throat. What he was doing felt so good and she didn't want him to stop. But he did. Taking her mouth once again.

He loved her taste.

And he couldn't get enough of it, which was why he was eating away at her mouth with a relentless hunger. He was driven by a need that was as primitive as time and as urgent as the desire to breathe. He could feel the rise and fall of her breasts pressed to his chest and could even feel the quivering of her thighs against his.

He hadn't had the time or inclination to get involved with a woman since moving to Royal. Brad's problems meant putting his social life on hold. He had been satisfied with that until Sheila had come along. She had kicked his hormones into gear, made him remember what it felt like to be hard up. But this was different. He'd never wanted a woman to this extreme.

And kissing her wasn't enough.

Keeping his mouth locked to hers, he walked her backward toward the sofa and when they reached it, he lowered her to it. Pulling his mouth away, he took a lick of her swollen lips before saying, "Tell me to stop now if you don't want what I'm about to give you."

She gazed up at him as if weighing his words and his eyes locked with hers. His gaze was practically drowning in the desire he saw in hers. And then he knew that she wanted him as much as he wanted her. But still, he was letting her call the shots. And if she decided in his favor, there was no turning back.

Instead of giving him an answer, she reached up and wrapped her arms around his neck and pulled his mouth back down to hers. He came willingly. Assuaging the hunger they both were feeling. At the same time, his hands were busy, unbuttoning her pajama top with deft fingers.

He pulled back from the kiss to look down at her and his breath caught in his throat. Her breasts were beautiful. Absolutely beautiful. He leaned down close to her ear and whispered, "I want to cherish you with my mouth, Sheila."

No man had ever said such a thing to her, Sheila thought, and immediately closed her eyes and drew in a deep breath when he immediately went for a breast, sucked a hardened nipple between his lips. She could feel her breasts swelling in his mouth. Her stomach clenched and she couldn't help moaning his name. She felt every part of her body stir to life with his touch.

Her response to his actions was instinctive. And when he took the tip of his tongue and began swirling around her nipple, and then grazing that same nipple with the edge of his teeth, she nearly came off the sofa.

She began shivering from the desire rushing through her body and when he moved to the next nipple, she felt every nerve ending in her breast come alive beneath his mouth. This was torture, plain and simple. And with each flick of his tongue she felt a pull, a tingling sensation between her legs.

As if he sensed the ache there, he pulled back slightly

and tugged her pj bottoms down her legs. Then he stared down at the juncture of her thighs when he saw she wasn't wearing panties. He uttered a sound that resembled a growl, and the next thing she knew he had shifted positions and lowered his mouth between her legs.

He went at her as if this had been his intent all along, using the tip of his tongue to stir a fervor within her, widening her thighs to delve deeper. What he was doing to her with his tongue should be outlawed. And he was taking his time, showing no signs that he was in a hurry. He was acting as if he had the entire night and intended to savor and get his fill. And she was helpless to do anything but rock her body against his mouth. The more she rocked, the deeper his tongue seemed to go.

And then she felt it, that first sign that her body was reaching a peak of tremendous pleasure that would seep through her pores, strip her of all conscious thought and swamp her with feelings she had never felt before. She held her breath, almost fighting what was to come, and when it happened she tried pushing his mouth away, but he only locked it onto her more. She threw her head back and moaned as sensation swept through her. She felt good. She felt alive. She felt as though her body no longer belonged to her.

And as the sensations continued to sprint through her, Zeke kept it up, pushing her more over the edge, causing a maelstrom of pleasure to engulf her; pleasure so keen it almost took her breath away. She began reveling in the feelings of contentment, although her body felt drained. It was then that he released her and slowly pulled back. With eyes laden with fulfillment, she watched as he quickly removed his own clothes and sheathed his erection in a condom. And then he returned to her. As if he wanted her body to get used to him, get to know him, he straddled her and gyrated his hips so that the tip of him made circles on her belly, before tracing an erotic path down to the area between her legs.

Sensuous pressure built once again inside her, starting at the base of her neck and escalating down. And when he eased between her womanly folds and slowly entered her, she called his name as his erection throbbed within her to the hilt. It was then that he began moving, thrusting in and out of her like as if this would be the last chance he had to do so, that she could feel her body come apart in the most sensuous way.

He stroked her for everything she was worth and then some, making her realize just what a generous lover he was. She locked her legs around him and he rocked deeper inside her. And then he touched a spot she didn't know existed and just in the nick of time, he lowered his mouth to hers to quell her scream as another orgasm hit.

Then his body bucked inside her several times, and he moaned into her mouth and she knew at that moment that both of them had gone beyond what they'd intended. But they couldn't turn back now even if they wanted to. He kept thrusting inside her, prolonging the orgasm they were sharing, and she knew at that moment this was meant to be. This night. The two of them together this way. There would be no regrets on her part. Only memories of what they were sharing now. Immense pleasure.

Entering Sheila's bedroom, Zeke's gaze touched on every single candle she had lit, bathing her bedroom in a very romantic glow. He had gotten a glimpse of her bedroom before, when he'd been in the room across the hall putting the crib together. Evidently she liked flowers, because her curtains and bedspread had a floral pattern.

He turned back the covers before placing her in the center of the bed. He joined her there and hoped Sunnie slept through the night as Sheila predicted she would. They had made a pit stop by the nursery to check on the baby and found her sleeping in spite of all the winds howling outside.

"Thanks for coming and checking on us," Sheila said, cuddling closer to him. He wrapped her into his arms, liking the feel of having her there. Her back was resting against his chest and her naked bottom nestled close to his groin.

"You don't have to thank me."

She glanced over her shoulder at him. "I don't?"

"No."

She smiled and closed her eyes, shifting her body to settle even more into his. He stayed awake and, lifting up on his elbows, he stared down at her. She was just as beautiful with her eyes closed as she was with them open. He then recalled what Brad had said about Sheila getting attached to Sunnie and could definitely see how that could happen.

He couldn't help wondering how she was going to handle it when Sunnie was taken away. And she would be taken away. Although Sunnie didn't belong to Brad, she did belong to someone. And if no one claimed her, she would eventually become a part of the system.

That was the one thing that had kept him out of trouble as a kid growing up, the fear of that very thing happening to him. Although he now knew his aunt would never have done such a thing, he hadn't known it then and had lived in constant fear that one day, if he did something wrong, his aunt would desert him in the same way his mother had.

But Clarisse Daniels had proven to be a better woman than her younger sister could ever be. A divorcée, which made her a single mother, she had raised both him and Alicia on a teacher's salary. At least child support had kicked in from Alicia's father every month. But neither his mother nor his father had ever contributed a penny to his upbringing. In fact, he'd found out later that his aunt had on several occasions actually given in to his mother's demand for money just to keep her from taking him away.

His father. He hadn't been completely honest with Sheila that day when he'd said he hadn't known his father. Mr. Travers was his father. He might not have known the man while growing up as Ezekiel "Zeke" Daniels, but he certainly knew his identity now. Matthew Travers. One of the richest men in Texas.

It seemed his mother had gotten knocked up by the man who hadn't believed her claim. In a way, considering what Zeke had heard, his father could have been one of two men. His mother hadn't known for certain which one had sired her son. She had gone after the wealthiest. Travers's attorney had talked her out of such foolishness and pretty much told her what would happen if she made her claim public. Evidently she took his threat seriously and he had grown up as Ezekiel Daniels, the son of Kristi Daniels. Father unknown. His birth certificate stated as much.

It was only while in college attending UT that there was a guy on campus who could have been his identical twin by the name of Colin Travers. When the two finally met, their resemblance was so uncanny it was unreal. Even Brad had approached the guy one day thinking it was him.

Zeke was willing to let the issue of their looks drop, but Colin wasn't. He went back to Houston, questioned his father and put together the pieces of what had happened between Matthew Travers and Kristi Daniels many years before, and a year or so before Travers had married Colin's mother.

When Zeke had been summoned to the Travers mansion, it was Brad who'd convinced him to go. It was there that he'd come face-to-face with the man who'd fathered him. The man, who after seeing him, was filled with remorse for not having believed Kristi Daniels's claim. The man who from that moment on intended to right a wrong, and make up to Zeke for all the years he hadn't been there for him. All the years he'd been denied. Abandoned.

He'd also found out that day that in addition to Colin, he had five other younger brothers and a sister. His siblings, along with their mother, Victoria, immediately accepted him as a Travers. But for some reason, Zeke had resisted becoming part of the Travers clan.

He'd always been a loner and preferred things staying that way. Although his siblings still kept in contact with him, especially Colin, who over the years had forged a close relationship with Zeke, he'd kept a distance between him and the old man. But his father was determined, regardless of Zeke's feelings on the matter, to build a relationship with him.

It was Brad and his aunt Clarisse who had been there for him during that difficult and confused time in his life. It was they who convinced him to take the last name his father wanted him to have and wear it proudly.

That's the reason why on his twenty-first birthday, he officially became Ezekiel *Travers*.

That's why he and Brad had such a strong friendship. And that was one of the main reasons his aunt meant the world to him. The first thing he'd done after being successful in his own right through lucrative investments was to buy Aunt Clarisse a house not far from the French Quarter. Alicia and her husband, both attorneys, didn't live too far away. He tried to go visit whenever he could. But now, he couldn't even consider going anywhere until he'd solved this case.

He glanced down at Sheila. And not without Sheila.

He immediately felt a tightening in his stomach. How could he even think something like that? He'd never taken a woman home to meet his family before. There had never been one he'd gotten that attached to, and he didn't plan to start doing so now.

He would be the first to say that tonight he and Sheila had enjoyed each other, but that's as far as things went. It just wasn't in his makeup to go further. Suddenly feeling as though he was suffocating and needed space, he eased away from Sheila and slid out of bed.

Tiptoeing across the hall, he went to where Sunnie was sleeping. She was lying on her stomach and sleeping peacefully. He wasn't sure what kind of future was in store for her, but he hope for her sake things worked out to her benefit.

All he knew was that the woman who'd given birth to the beautiful baby didn't deserve her.

Seven

"You want us to go to your place?" Sheila asked to make sure she'd heard Zeke correctly.

They had awakened to the forecaster's grim news that Hurricane Spencer was still hovering in the gulf. And although Royal was not directly in its path, if the storm did hit land, there would be a lot of wind and rain for the next day or so. The local news media had further indicated that although the electrical company was working around the clock, certain areas of town would remain without power for a while. Meadowland was one of them.

"Yes, I think it would be for the best for now—especially since you don't know when your power will be restored. I have a generator in case the power goes out at my house."

Sheila nibbled on her bottom lip. What he was offering made sense, but she was so used to having her own place, her own stuff. She glanced over at Sunnie, who was sitting in the middle of the kitchen table in her car seat. She had just been fed and was happy. And she hadn't seemed bothered by seeing Zeke. In fact, it seemed as if she smiled when she saw him.

"Sheila?"

"I was just thinking of all the stuff I'd have to pack up and carry with us."

"We can manage. Besides, I have my truck."

How convenient, she thought. She knew his idea made perfect sense, but going over to his place meant leaving her comfort zone. "Sunnie has gotten used to being here," she said.

"I understand, but as long as you're within her sight, she'll be fine."

Sheila nibbled on her bottom lip as she gave her attention back to the baby. Yes, Sunnie would be fine, but she wasn't sure she would be. Waking up in Zeke's arms hadn't been exactly what she'd planned to happen. But it had been so natural. Just like the lovemaking that had followed before they'd heard Sunnie through the monitor that morning.

She had just finished feeding Sunnie when Zeke had dropped what she considered a bomb. She had been thinking how, in a nice way, to suggest they rethink what had happened between them last night and give each other space to do so, when his idea had been just the opposite. Moving her and Sunnie into his house until the storm passed was not giving them space.

Deciding to come out and say what she'd been thinking, she glanced back over at Zeke. He was sitting across the kitchen, straddling a chair. "What about last night?"

He held her gaze. "What about it?"

Sheila's heart thumped hard in her chest. "W-we slept together and we should not have," she stammered, wishing she hadn't been so blunt, but not knowing what else she could have said to broach the subject and let him know her feelings on the matter.

"It was inevitable."

Her eyes widened in surprise at his comeback. "I don't think it was. Why do you?"

"Because I wanted you from the first and I picked up on the vibes that you wanted me, too."

What vibes? "I was attracted to you from the first, I admit that," she said. "But I wasn't sending off vibes."

"Yes, you were."

Had she unconsciously emitted vibes as he claimed? She tried to recall such a time and—

"Remember that day you woke me up when I'd fallen asleep on your sofa?"

She nodded, remembering. They had stared at each other for the longest time. "Yes, I remember."

"You blushed but wouldn't tell me what you were thinking, what was going through your mind to make you do so."

"So you assumed…"

"No, I knew. I think I can read you pretty well."

"You think so?"

"Yes. I can probably guess with certainty the times we've been together when your thoughts of me were sexual."

Could he really? She didn't like that and to hear him say it actually irritated her. "Look, Zeke, I'm not sure about the women you're used to getting involved with, but—"

"But you are different from them," he finished for her. "And I agree you're different in a positive way."

"We've known each other less than a week," she reminded him.

"Yes, but we've shared more in that time than a lot of people share in a lifetime. Especially last night. The connection between us was unreal."

Sheila immediately thought of her friend Emily Burroughs. If she could claim ever having a best friend it would have to be Emily. They had been roommates in college. And she believed they had a special friendship that would have gotten even stronger over the years… if Emily hadn't died. Her friend had died of ovarian cancer at the young age of twenty-three.

Sheila had been with Emily during her final days. Emily hadn't wanted to go to hospice, preferring to die at home in her own bed. And she had wanted Sheila there with her for what they'd known would be their last slumber party. It was then Emily had shared that although she wasn't a virgin, she'd never made out with a guy and felt one gigantic explosion; she'd never heard bells and whistles. Emily had never felt the need to scream. She had died not experiencing any of that. And last night Sheila had encountered everything that Emily hadn't in her lifetime.

"Do you regret last night, Sheila?"

His question intruded into her thoughts and she glanced back over at him, wondering how she could get him to understand that she was a loner. Always had been and probably always would be. She didn't take rejection well, and every time the people she loved the most rejected her, intentionally put distance between them, was a swift blow to her heart.

"No, Zeke, but I've learned over the years not to get attached to people. My mom has been married five times and my sister from my father's first marriage doesn't want to be my sister because my mother caused her father pain."

He frowned. "You didn't have anything to do with that."

She chuckled. "Try telling Lois that. She blames both me and my mother and I was only four when they split."

"Did you talk to your father about it?"

She shook her head. "When Dad left, he never wanted to see me or my mother again. I guess I would have been a reminder of what she did. She cheated on him."

"But it wasn't your fault."

"No, it wasn't," she said, wiping the baby's mouth. "And I grew up believing that one day one of them, hopefully both, would realize that. Neither did. Dad died five years ago. He was a very wealthy man and over the years he did do right by me financially—my mother saw to that. But when he died, he intended to let me know how much I didn't mean to him by leaving Lois everything. I wasn't even mentioned in his will."

She paused a moment, glanced away from him to look out the window as she relived the pain. And then back at him and said, "It's not that I wanted any of his worldly possessions, mind you. It was the principle of the thing. Just acknowledging me in some way as his daughter would have been nice."

Sheila glanced over at Sunnie, who was staring over at her, as if she understood the nature of what she'd said, of what she was sharing with Zeke. She then wondered why she had shared such a thing with him.

Maybe telling him would help him to realize that she could get attached to him, and why she couldn't let that happen.

"So, no, I don't regret last night. It was too beautiful, too earth-shattering and mind-blowing to regret. But I have to be realistic and accept that I don't do involvement very well. I get attached easily. You might want a casual affair, but a part of me would long for something more."

"Something I can't give you," he said gently. The sound of his husky voice floated across the room to her.

"Precisely," she said, nodding her head while thinking that he did understand.

"I could say I won't touch you again, even if we spend time together."

She would have taken his words to heart if at that moment a smile hadn't curved his lips. "Yes, you could say that," she agreed.

"But I'd be lying. Mainly because you are temptation."

"Temptation?" she asked, and couldn't help chuckling at that.

"Yes."

She shook her head. She had been called many things but never temptation. "You can see me in the garden with an apple?"

His eyes seemed to darken. "Yes, and very much naked."

Sensing the change in the tone of his voice—it had gone from a deep husky to a seductive timbre—she decided maybe they needed to change the subject. "How is the case coming?"

Zeke recognized her ploy to change the subject. She had reservations about sleeping with him again and he could understand that. But what she needed to understand was that there were some things a man and a woman could not ignore. Blatant sexual chemistry was one of them—it pretty much headed the list. And that was what existed between them, connecting more than just the dots.

Making love to her and waking up with her last night had affected him in a way he didn't quite comprehend, and because he didn't understand it, he wasn't ready, or willing, to walk away.

And when she'd tried explaining to him why she preferred not getting involved in a relationship for fear of getting attached, it was like hearing his own personal reservations. He had this apprehension of letting any woman get too close for fear she would do to him the very thing his mother had done. Walk away and leave him high and dry…and take his heart with her. He'd been there and done that and would never go that way again.

She was protecting her heart the way he was protecting his, so they were on the same page there. Maybe he should tell her that. Then maybe he shouldn't. Opening himself up to anyone wasn't one of his strong points. He was a private person. Few people got to know the real Ezekiel Travers. Brad and his other college friend and Royal resident, Christopher Richards, knew the real Zeke. And he felt comfortable being himself around Darius Franklin. Over the past year, while working through the terms of their partnership, he had gotten to know Darius, a man he highly respected. And he thought Summer was the perfect wife for Darius.

One night over dinner Darius and Summer had shared their story. How things had ended for them due to a friend's betrayal. They had gotten reunited seven years later and intended never to let anything or anyone come between them again. He was convinced that kind of love could only be found by a few people. He would never think about holding out for a love that sure and pure for himself.

He decided to go with Sheila's change of subject. "The case is coming along. I'm still following up possible leads."

He told her about his conversations with Rali Tariq and Arthur Moran and their admissions that they too had received blackmail letters.

"You mean they received blackmail letters claiming they fathered babies, as well?"

"Not exactly. Both are married men and they received letters threatening to expose them as having cheated on their wives, which they both deny doing. But both knew doctored pictures could have shown another story. It would have been embarrassing for their families while they tried to prove their innocence."

Sheila shook her head as she took Sunnie out of the car seat. "But knowing Bradford Price wasn't the only one who got a blackmail letter gives legitimacy to your his claim that he's not Sunnie's father, and it's all a hoax to extract money from TCC members, right?"

"In a way, yes. But you'll still have some who have their doubts. The paternity test would clear him for sure." He saw a thoughtful look in her eye. Clearing Brad also meant that Sheila would have to give Sunnie up.

Zeke stood and glanced out the window. "It's stopped raining. If we're going to my place we need to do so before it starts up again."

She frowned. "I never said I was going to your place with you."

He slowly crossed the room to her. "I know. But considering everything, even your apprehension about spending time with me, is there a reason you should subject Sunnie to another night in a house without power?"

Sheila swallowed, knowing there it was. The one person she couldn't deny. Sunnie. She looked down at the baby she held in her arms. In the end it would always be what was best for Sunnie. Right now she was all the little girl had. And she would always put her needs first. Last night hadn't been so bad, but it was November; even with fire in the fireplace, the house was beginning to feel drafty. And she couldn't risk the baby catching a cold all because she couldn't resist a tall, dark, handsome and well-built man name Zeke Travers.

She looked at Zeke, met his gaze. "Will you promise me something?"

"What?"

"That while we're at your place you won't…"

He took a step closer. "I won't what?"

She nibbled on her bottom lip. "Try seducing me into sleeping with you again."

He studied her features for a moment and then he reached out and caressed her cheek with the back of his hand while he continued to hold her gaze. "Sorry, sweetheart, that is one promise I won't make you," he said in a low, husky tone. He took a step back. "I'll start loading up Sunnie's stuff in my truck."

Sheila held her breath until he walked out of the room.

Zeke pretended not to notice how well Sheila inter-acted with Sunnie as he loaded the last of the baby items into his truck. They would probably be at his place only a day at the most. But with everything Sheila had indicated she needed to take, you would think they were moving in for a full year. He chuckled. He had no complaints. He had a huge house and lately he'd noticed how lonely it would seem at times.

He heard the baby chuckle and glanced back over at her. He couldn't tell who was giggling more, Sunnie or Sheila, and quickly decided it was a tie. He pushed his Stetson back off his head, thinking, as well as knowing, she would make a great mother. She always handled Sunnie with care, as if she was the most precious thing she'd ever touched.

She glanced over at him, caught him staring and gave him a small smile. The one he returned had a lot more depth than the one she'd given him and he understood why. She still had misgivings about spending time at his place. He didn't blame her too much. He had every intention of finishing what had gotten started between them last night. By not agreeing to her request not to get her into his bed, he'd pretty much stated what his intentions were and he wasn't backing down.

But as he'd told her, there was no way he could make her that promise. It would have died a quick death on his lips as soon as he'd made it. And the one thing his Aunt Clarisse had taught him not to do was lie. She'd always said lies could come back to haunt you. They would catch up with you at the worst possible time. And he had believed her.

He moved from around the back of the truck. "Ready to go?"

He could tell she wasn't ready. But she widened her smile a little and said, "Yes. Let me get Sunnie into her seat."

He watched as she strapped the baby in her car seat, again paying attention to every little detail of Sunnie's security and comfort. He stepped back as she closed the door, and then he opened the passenger door for her and watched how easily she slid in across the leather. Nice, he thought. Especially when he caught a glimpse of bare thigh. He'd never given a thought to how much he appreciated seeing a woman in a skirt until now.

He got into the truck, backed out her yard and was halfway down the road when she glanced over at him. "I want to use one of your guest rooms, Zeke."

"All right."

Zeke kept looking straight ahead, knowing she had glanced over at him, trying to decipher the quickness of his answer. She would discover soon enough that physical attraction was a very powerful thing. And now that they'd experienced just how things could be between them, it wouldn't be that easy to give it up. And it just so happened that his bedroom was right across the hall from the guest room he intended to put her in.

"I can make a pit stop and grab something to eat. What would you like?" he asked her.

"Oh, anything. I'm not that hungry."

He looked over at her when he brought the car to a stop at a traffic light. "Maybe not now, but you'll probably be hungry later."

And he didn't add that she should eat something to keep her strength for the plans he had for her after she put the baby to bed for the night. He felt a deep stirring inside him. There was something about her scent that made him want to mate. And mate they would again. His peace of mind and everything male within him was depending on it. He couldn't wait for night to come.

But for now he would pretend to go along with anything she thought she wanted, and making sure by the time it was over she'd be truly and thoroughly convinced what she wanted was him. Usually, when it came to women, he didn't like playing games. He liked to be honest, but he didn't consider what he was doing as playing a game. What he was doing was trying to keep his sanity. He honestly didn't think she knew just how luscious she was. Maybe he hadn't shown her enough last night. Evidently he needed to give her several more hints. And he would do so gladly. He shifted in his seat when he felt tightness in the crotch of his pants while thinking how such a thing would be accomplished.

"You don't mind if I pull into that chicken place, do you?" he asked, gesturing to a KFC.

"No, I guess you're a growing boy and have to eat sometime," she said, smiling over at him.

Growing boy was right, and there was no need to tell her what part of him seemed to be outgrowing all the others at the moment.

Sheila glanced around the bedroom she was given. Zeke had set up Sunnie's bed in a connecting room. She loved his home. It looked like the perfect place for a family.

She pulled a romance novel out of her bag before sliding into bed. When they arrived here, she had helped him get everything inside. After that was done they had both sat down to enjoy the fried-chicken lunch he'd purchased. After that was done he had gone outside to check on things. The fierce winds had knocked down several branches and Zeke and his men had taken the time to clean up the debris. While he was outside, Sheila and Sunnie had made themselves at home.

So far he had been the perfect gentleman and had even volunteered to watch the baby while she had taken a shower. Sunnie had gotten used to seeing him and didn't cry when he held her. In fact, it seemed that she was giving him as many smiles as she was giving to her.

Now Sunnie was down for the night and it had started raining again. Sheila could hear the television downstairs and knew Zeke was still up. She thought it would be better for her to remain in her room and read. She would see him in the morning and that was soon enough to suit her.

She had been reading for about an hour or so when she decided to go to the connecting room to check on Sunnie. Although the baby now slept through the night, Sheila checked on her periodically. Sunnie had a tendency to kick off her bedcovers while she slept.

Sheila tiptoed into the room. Already the scent of baby powder drenched the air and she smiled. Sunnie's presence was definitely known. When Sheila had come downstairs after taking a shower, Zeke had been holding the baby in his arms and was standing at the window. From Sunnie's giggles she could tell the baby had enjoyed seeing the huge raindrops roll down the windowpane.

It had been a spine-tilting moment to see him standing there in his bare feet, shirtless with his jeans riding low on his hips. A tall, sexy hulk of a man with a tiny baby in his arms. A baby he was holding as gently as if she was his.

She had watched them and thought that he would make a wonderful father. She wondered if he wanted kids one day. He had talked about his cousin's twins and she knew he didn't have an aversion to kids like some men did. Crawford would freeze up whenever the mention of a baby entered their conversation. That had been one topic not open for discussion between them.

Pulling the covers back over Sunnie's chubby legs, Sheila was about to exit when she felt another presence in the room. She turned quickly and saw Zeke sitting in the wingback chair with his legs stretched out in front of him. He was sitting silently and watching her, saying nothing.

The glow of the moon flowing in through the curtains highlighted his features and the look she saw in his eyes said it all. She fought not to be moved by that look, but it was more powerful than anything she'd ever encountered. It was like a magnetic force, pulling her in, weakening her, filling her with a need she had been fighting since awakening that morning.

She wished she could stop her heart from beating a mile a minute, or stop her nipples from pressing hard against her nightgown. Then there was the heat she felt between her legs; the feeling was annoying as well as arousing.

Then he stood and she had to tilt her head back to look at him. In the moonlight she saw him crook his finger for her to follow him into the hall. Knowing it was best they not speak in the room to avoid awakening Sunnie, she followed.

"I didn't know you were in there with Sunnie," she said softly.

He leaned against the wall. "I went in there to check on her…and to wait for you."

A knot formed in Sheila's throat. "Wait for me?" He seemed to have inched closer. She inhaled his masculine scent into her nostrils and her nipples stiffened even more.

"Yes. I knew you would be coming to check on Sunnie sooner or later. And I decided to sit it out until you did."

She shifted her body when she felt a tingling sensation at the juncture of her thighs. "Why would you be waiting for me?"

She was warned by the smile that tilted his lips at the same time as he slipped an arm around her waist and said, "I was waiting to give you this."

He leaned his mouth down to hers. And instinctively, she went on tiptoe to meet him halfway.

This was well worth the wait, Zeke thought as he deepened the kiss. There was nothing like being inside her mouth. Nothing like holding her in his arms. Nothing like hearing the sound of her moaning deep in his ear.

And he had waited. From the moment she had gone upstairs to put the baby to bed, he had waited for her to come back downstairs. She hadn't done so. Instead, she had called down to him from the top of the stairs to tell him good-night.

He had smiled at her ploy to put distance between them, and he put a plan into action. He figured there was no way she would settle in for the night without checking on Sunnie. So he had closed up things downstairs and gone upstairs and waited.

The wait was over.

She was where he wanted her to be. Here in his arms where he needed her to be. But he needed her someplace else, as well. His bed. Lifting his mouth from hers, he gazed down into the darkness of her eyes and whispered against her moist lips, "I need to make love to you, sweetheart. I have to get inside you."

Sheila nearly moaned at the boldness of his statement. And the desire she saw in his dark gaze was so fierce, so ferocious, that she could feel an intensity stirring within her that she'd never felt before. His need was rousing hers.

She reached up and wrapped her arms around his neck, brought her mouth close to his and whispered thickly, "And I want you inside me, too." And she meant it. Had felt each and every word she had spoken. The throbbing between her legs had intensified from the hardness of him pressing against her and she was feeling him. Boy, was she feeling him.

Before she could release her next breath, he swept her off her feet and into his arms and headed across the hall to his bedroom.

Nothing, Zeke thought, had prepared him for meeting a woman like Sheila. She hadn't come on to him like others. Had even tried keeping her distance. But the chemistry had been too great and intensified each and every time they were within a foot of each other.

The last time they'd made love had been almost too much for his mind and body to handle. And now he could only imagine the outcome of this mating. But he needed it the way he needed to breathe.

He placed her on the bed and before she could get settled, he had whipped the nightgown from her body. She looked up at him and smiled. "Hey, you're good at that."

"At what?" he asked, stepping back to remove his own clothes.

"Undressing a woman."

As he put on a condom, he glanced at her. She was the only woman he wanted to undress. The only woman he enjoyed undressing. The only woman he wanted to make love to. Suddenly, upon realizing what his mind had just proclaimed, he forced it free of such an assertion. He could and never would be permanently tied to any one woman. That was the last thing he wanted to think about now or ever.

He moved back toward the bed. The way she was gazing at every inch of his body made him aware of just what she was seeing, and just what he wanted to give her. What he wanted them to share. What he intended them to savor.

He stopped at the edge of the bed and returned her gaze with equal intensity. Moonlight pouring in through his window shone on her nakedness. There she was. Beautiful. Bare. His eyes roamed over her uplifted breasts, creamy brown skin, small waist, luscious thighs, gorgeous hips and then to the apex of her thighs.

"Zeke."

She said his name before he even touched her. She rose on the bed to meet him. The moment their lips fused, it was on. Desire burst like a piece of hot glass within him, cutting into his very core. Blazing heat rushed through his veins with every stroke of his tongue that she returned.

He lowered her to the mattress and pulled back from the kiss, needed the taste of her and proceeded to kiss her all over. He gloried in the way she trembled beneath his mouth, but he especially liked the taste of her wet center, and proved just how much he enjoyed it.

She came in an explosion that shook the bed and he cupped her bottom, locked his mouth to her while those erotic sensations slashed through her. And when his tongue found a section of her G-spot and went after it as if it would be his last meal, she shuddered uncontrollably.

It was only then that he pulled back and placed his body over hers. "I like your taste," he whispered huskily. He eased inside her, stretching her as he went deep. Her womb was still aching and he could feel it. Already she wanted more and he intended to give her what she wanted.

He began thrusting inside her, thinking he would never tire of doing so. He was convinced there would never come a time when he wouldn't want to make love to her. He slid his hands beneath her hips to lift her off the bed, needing to go even deeper. And when he had reached the depth he wanted, he continued to work her flesh. Going in and out of her relentlessly.

He threw his head back when she moaned his name and he felt her inner muscles clench him, hold him tight, trying to pull every single thing out of him. And he gave in to her demand in one guttural moan, feeling the veins in his neck almost bursting in the process. Coming inside a woman had never felt this right before. This monumental. This urgent.

He rode her hard as his body continued to burst into one hell of an explosion, his shudders combined with hers, nearly shaking the bed from the frame. This was lovemaking at its best. The kind that would leave you mindless. Yet still wanting more. When had he become so greedy?

He would try to figure out the answer to that later. Right now the only thing he wanted to dwell on were the feelings swamping him, ripping into every part of his body, taking him for all it was worth and then some. It had to be the most earth-shattering orgasm he'd ever experienced. More intense than the ones last night, and he'd thought those were off the charts.

And he knew moments later when his body finally withdrew from hers to slump beside her, weak as water, that it would always be that way with them. She would always be the one woman who would be his temptation. The one woman he would not be able to resist.

Eight

Zeke and Sheila were aware that the power had returned to her section of town. Yet neither brought up the subject of her returning home. Four days later and she was still spending her days and nights in Zeke's home and loving every moment of it.

The rain had stopped days ago and sunshine was peeking out over the clouds. Those sunny days were her favorite. That's when she would take the baby outside and push her around in the stroller. Zeke's property was enormous and she and Sunnie enjoyed exploring as much of it as they could. Sunnie was fascinated by the horses and would stare at them as if she was trying to figure out what they were.

Then there were the nights when she would fall asleep in Zeke's arms after having made love. He was the most generous lover and made her feel special each and every time he touched her. She was always encouraged by his bold sexuality, where he would take their lovemaking to the hilt. When it came to passion, Crawford had always been low-key. Zeke was just the opposite. He liked making love in or out of bed. And he especially enjoyed quickies. She smiled, thinking she was enjoying them, too.

Usually Zeke worked in his office downstairs for a few hours while she played games with Sunnie, keeping her entertained. Then when he came out of his office, he would spend time with them. One day he had driven them to a nearby park, and on another day he took them to the zoo.

On this particular day Zeke had gone into his office in town to work on a few files when his house phone rang. Usually he received calls on his cell phone, and Sheila decided not to answer it. The message went to his voice mail, which she heard.

"Hi, Ezekiel. This is Aunt Clarisse. I'm just calling to see how you're doing. I had a doctor's appointment today and he says I'm doing fine. And how is that baby someone left on the doorstep and claiming it's Brad's? I know you said you were going to keep an eye on the baby real close, so how is that going? Knowing you, you're probably not letting that baby out of your sight until you find out the truth one way or another..."

A knot twisted in Sheila's stomach. Was that why she was still here? Is that why Zeke hadn't mentioned anything about taking her home? Why he was making love to her each night? Was his main purpose for showing interest in her to keep his eye on Sunnie?

She fought back the tears that threatened to fall from her eyes. What other reason could there be? Had she really thought—had she hoped—that there could be another reason? Hadn't she learned her lesson yet?

Hadn't her father, mother and sister taught her that in this life she had no one? When all was said and done, she would be left high and dry. Alone.

Her only excuse for letting her guard down was that usually to achieve their goal of alienating her the ones she loved would try putting distance between them. That's why her father never came to visit, why Lois preferred keeping her from Atlanta and why her mother never invited her to visit her and her husbands.

But Zeke had been the exception. He had wanted to keep her close. Now she knew the reason why.

She drew in a deep breath. When Zeke returned she would tell him she wanted to go home. He would wonder why, but frankly she didn't care. Nor would she tell him. It was embarrassing and humiliating enough for her to know the reason.

One day she would learn her lesson.

Zeke glanced over at Sheila, surprised. "You want to go home?"

She continued packing up the baby's items. "Yes. The only reason Sunnie and I are here is because of your generosity in letting us stay due to the power being out at my place. It's back on now and there's no reason for us to remain here any longer."

He bit back the retort that she'd known the power was back on days ago, yet she hadn't been in a hurry to leave…just as he hadn't been in a hurry for her to go. What happened to make her want to take off? He rubbed the back of his neck. "Is something going on that I need to know about, Sheila?"

She glanced up. "No. I just want to go home."

He continued to stare at her. He'd known she'd eventually want to return home. Hell, he had to be realistic here. "Fine, we can take some of Sunnie's things now and you can come back for the rest later on in the week."

"I prefer taking all Sunnie's items now. There's no reason for me to come back. "

That sounded much like a clean break to him. Why? "Okay, then I'd better start loading stuff up." He walked out of the room.

Sheila glanced at the door Zeke had just walked out of, suddenly feeling alone. She might as well get used to it again. Sunnie's days were numbered with her either way. And now that she knew what Zeke was about, it would be best if she cut the cord now.

In the other room Zeke was taking down the baby bed he'd gotten used to seeing. Why was he beginning to feel as if he was losing his best friend? Why was the feeling of abandonment beginning to rear its ugly head again?

Waking up with her beside him each morning had meant more to him than it had to her evidently. Having both Sheila and Sunnie in his home had been the highlight of his life for the past four days. He had gotten used to them being around and had enjoyed the time they'd spent together. A part of him had assumed the feelings were mutual. Apparently he'd assumed wrong.

A short while later he had just finished taking the bed down, when his cell phone rang. He pulled it out of his back pocket. "Yes?"

"I just got a call from my attorney," Brad said. "There's a possibility I might get the results of the paternity test as early as tomorrow. Hell, I hope so. I need to get on with my life. Get on with the election."

"That's good to hear." At least it would be good for

Brad, but not so good for Sheila. Either way, she would be turning the baby over to someone, whether it was Brad or the system. And the way he saw it, there was a one-hundred-percent chance it would be the system.

"Let me know when you get the results," he said to Brad.

His best friend chuckled. "Trust me. You'll be the first to know."

A few hours later back at her place Sheila stood at the window and watched Zeke pull off. He had stayed just long enough to put up the crib. No doubt he'd picked up on her rather cold attitude, but he hadn't questioned her about it. Nor had he indicated he would be returning.

However, since his sole purpose in seeing her was to spy on her, she figured he would return eventually. When he did, it would be on her terms and not his. She had no problem with him wanting to make sure Sunnie was well taken care of, but he would not be using her to do so.

She turned from the window, deciding it was time to take Sunnie upstairs for her bath, when she heard the phone ringing. She crossed the room to pick it up. "Hello?"

"Ms. Hopkins?"

"Yes?"

"This is Ms. Talbert from Social Services."

Sheila felt an immediate knot in her stomach. "Yes?"

"We received notification from the lab that the results of Bradford Price's paternity test might be available earlier than we expected. I thought we'd let you know that."

Sheila swallowed as she glanced across the room at Sunnie. She was sitting in her swing, laughing as she played with the toys attached to it.

"Does Mr. Price know?"

"I would think so. His attorney was contacted earlier today."

She drew in a deep breath. It would be safe to assume that if Bradford Price knew then Zeke knew. Why hadn't he mentioned this to her? Prepared her?

"Ms. Hopkins?"

The woman reclaimed her attention. "Yes?"

"Do you have any questions for us?"

"No."

"Okay, then. How is the baby doing?"

Sheila glanced over at Sunnie. "She's fine."

"That's good. I'll call you sometime this week to let you know when to bring the baby in."

"All right." Sheila hung up the phone and forced the tears back.

Zeke entered his house convinced something in Sheila's attitude toward him had changed. But what and why?

He went straight into the kitchen to grab a beer, immediately feeling how lonely his house was. It had taken Sheila and the baby being here for him to realize there was a difference between a house and a home. This place was a house.

He had drunk his beer and was about to go upstairs when he noticed a blinking light on his phone. He crossed the room to retrieve his messages and smiled upon hearing his aunt's voice. Moments later a frown touched his lips. When had his aunt called? He played back the message to extract the time. She had called around noon when Sheila had been here. Had she heard it?

He rubbed his hands down his face, knowing the assumptions that would probably come into her mind if she had. Sunnie was not the reason he'd been spending time with her. But after hearing his aunt's message, she might think that it was.

He moved to the sofa to recall everything between them since returning home that day. Even on the car ride back to her place she hadn't said more than a few words. Although the words had been polite, and he hadn't detected anger or irritation in them, he'd known something was bothering her. At first he'd figured since this was the beginning of the second week, she was getting antsy over Sunnie's fate. He had tried engaging her in conversation, but to no avail.

He drew in a deep breath. Did she know that she had come to mean something to him? He chuckled. *Hell, man, how could she know when you're just realizing such a thing yourself?* Zeke knew at that moment that he had done with Sheila the very thing he hadn't wanted to do with any woman. He had fallen in love with her.

He didn't have to wonder how such a thing happened. Spending time with her had made him see what he was missing in his life. He had enjoyed leaving and coming home knowing she was here waiting for him. And at night when they retired, it was as if his bed was where she belonged.

He had thought about bringing up the subject of them trying their luck dating seriously. But he had figured they would have the opportunity to do that after everything with Sunnie was over. He envisioned them taking things slow and building a solid relationship. But now it looked as if that wouldn't be happening.

He then thought about the call he'd gotten from Brad, indicating the test results might be arriving sooner than later. He probably should have mentioned it to her, but after seeing her melancholy mood, he'd decided to keep the information to himself. The last thing he wanted her to start doing was worry about having to give up the baby she'd gotten attached to.

A part of him wanted to get in his car and go over to her place and tell her she had made wrong assumptions about his reason for wanting to be with her. But he figured he would give her space tonight. At some point tomorrow he would be seeing her, and hopefully they would be able to sit down and do some serious talking.

He stood from the sofa, when his cell phone rang. He quickly pulled it off his belt hoping it was Sheila, and then grimaced when he saw the caller was his father. Matthew Travers was determined not to let his oldest son put distance between them as Zeke often tried to do.

The old man made a point of calling often, and if Zeke got the notion not to accept the call, Matthew Travers wasn't opposed to sending one of his offspring to check on their oldest sibling. Hell, the old man had shown up on his doorstep a time or two himself. Zeke had learned the hard way his father was a man who refused to be denied anything he wanted.

Zeke shook his head thinking that must be a Travers trait, because he felt the same way about certain things. He was definitely feeling that way about Sheila. "Hello?"

"How are you doing, son?"

Zeke drew in a deep relaxing breath. That was always the way the old man began the conversation with him, referring to him as his son. Letting Zeke know he considered him as such.

Zeke sat back down on the sofa and stretched his legs out in front of him. "I'm doing fine, Dad."

At times it still sounded strange referring to Matthew

Travers as "Dad," even after twelve years. They hadn't talked in a while and he had a feeling that today his father was in a talkative mood.

The next day Zeke got to the office early, intending to follow up a few leads. Regardless of whether Brad was cleared of being Sunnie's father, there was still someone out there who'd set up an extortion scheme and had made several members of the TCC his or her victims.

He hoped he would be able to call it a day at Global Securities by five and hightail it over to Sheila's place. He hadn't been able to sleep for thinking about her last night. And he hadn't liked sleeping in his bed alone. Those days she'd spent with him had definitely changed his life.

He sat down at his desk remembering the conversation he'd had with his father. His father still wasn't overjoyed that Zeke had turned down the position of chief of security of Travers Enterprises to come work here with Darius. As he'd tried explaining to the old man, he preferred living in a small town, and moving from Austin to Houston would not have given him that.

And had he not moved to Royal, he thought further, *he would not have met Sheila.*

A few hours later while sitting at his desk with his sleeves rolled up and mulling over a file, his intercom buzzed with a call from his secretary. "Yes, Mavis?"

"Mr. Price and his attorney are here and want to see you."

Zeke glanced at the clock on his desk, a sterling-silver exclusive from his cousin. He frowned, not believing it was almost four in the afternoon. He couldn't help wondering why Brad and his attorney would be dropping by. "Please send them in."

Seconds later the door flew open and an angry Brad walked in followed by Alan Nelson, Brad's attorney. Zeke took one look at a furious Brad and a flustered Alan and knew something was wrong. "What the hell is going on?" he asked.

"This!" Brad said, tossing a document in the middle of Zeke's desk. "Alan just got it. It's a copy of the results of the paternity test and it's claiming that I'm that baby's father."

Sheila hung up the phone. It was Ms. Talbert again. She had called to say the results of the paternity test were in. Although the woman couldn't share the results with her, she told her that she would call back later that day or early tomorrow with details about when and where Sheila was to drop off the baby.

Sheila felt her body trembling inside. She was a nurse, so she should have known not to get attached to a patient. Initially, she had treated Sunnie as someone who'd been placed in her care. But that theory had died the moment that precious little girl had gazed up at her with those beautiful hazel eyes.

The baby hadn't wanted much. She just wanted to be loved and belong to someone. Sheila had certainly understood that, since those were the very things she wanted for herself. She hoped that Sunnie had a better chance at it than she'd had.

But not if she ends up in the system. And that thought bothered Sheila most of all. A part of her wanted to call Zeke, but she knew she couldn't do that. He hadn't gotten attached to her the way she had to him. Oh, he had gotten attached to her all right, but for all the wrong reasons.

She moved over toward the baby. Their time was

limited and she intended to spend as much quality time as she could with Sunnie. Although the baby was only five months old, she wanted her to feel loved and cherished. Because deep in Sheila's heart, she was.

"Calm down, Brad." Zeke then glanced over at Alan. "Will you please tell me what's going on?" he asked Brad's attorney.

Brad dropped down in the chair opposite Zeke's desk, and Zeke could tell the older man seemed relieved. There was no doubt in Zeke's mind that once Alan had delivered the news to Brad he'd wished he hadn't.

The man took out a handkerchief and wiped sweat off his brow before saying, "The paternity report shows a genetic link between Mr. Price and the baby."

Zeke lifted a brow. "Meaning?"

"It means that although there's a link, it's inconclusive as to whether he is Jane Doe's father."

Zeke cringed at Alan's use of the name Jane Doe for Sunnie. "Her name is Sunnie, Alan."

The man looked confused. "What?"

"The baby's name is Sunnie. And as far as what you're saying, we still don't know one way or the other?"

"No, but again, there is that genetic link," Alan reiterated.

Zeke released a frustrated sigh. He then turned his attention to Brad. "Brad, I know you recall not having been sexually involved with a woman during the time Sunnie would have been conceived, but did you at any time donate your sperm to a bank or anyplace like that?"

"Of course not!"

"Just asking. I knew a few guys who did so when we were in college," Zeke said.

"Well, I wasn't one of them." Brad stood up. "What am I going to do? If word of this gets out I might as well kiss the TCC presidency goodbye."

Zeke knew the word would probably get out. He'd found out soon enough that in Royal, like a number of small towns, people had a tendency to thrive on gossip, especially when it involved the upper crust of the city.

"Who contacted you about the results?" Zeke asked Alan.

"That woman at Social Services," Alan replied. "She's the one who called yesterday afternoon as well, letting me know there was a chance the results would be arriving sooner than expected. I called Brad and informed him of such."

Zeke nodded. And Brad had called him. "Did she mention she would be telling anyone else?"

"No, other than the woman who has custody of Jane Doe." Upon seeing Zeke's frown, he quickly said, "I mean Sunnie."

Zeke was immediately out of his chair. "She called Sheila Hopkins?"

"Yes, if that's the name of the woman keeping the baby. I'm sure she's not going to tell her the results of the test, only that the results are in," Alan replied. "Is there a problem?"

Yes, Zeke saw a problem but didn't have time to explain anything to the two men. "I need to go," he said, grabbing his Stetson and jacket and heading for the door.

"What's wrong?" Brad asked, getting to his feet and watching him dash off in a mad rush.

"I'll call you," Zeke said over his shoulder, and then he was out the door.

* * *

Sheila heard a commotion outside her window and, shifting Sunnie to her hip, she moved in that direction. Pushing the curtain aside, she watched as Summer tried corralling a group of pink flamingos down the street.

She had heard about the Helping Hands Shelter's most recent fundraiser. Someone had come up with the idea of the pink flamingos. The plan was that the recipient of the flamingos had to pay money to the charity for the opportunity to pass them on to the next unsuspecting victim, and then the cycle would start all over again.

Sunnie was making all kinds of excited noises seeing the flamingos, and the sound almost brought more tears to Sheila's eyes, knowing the day would come when she wouldn't hear that sound again. She knew she had to get out of her state of funk. But it was hard doing so.

She moved from the window when Summer continued to herd the flamingos down the street. Sheila was glad her friend hadn't ditched the flamingos on her. She had enough to deal with and passing on pink flamingos was the last thing she had time for.

She glanced down at Sunnie. "Okay, precious, it's dinnertime for you."

A short while later, after Sunnie had eaten, Sheila had given her a bath and put her to bed. The baby was usually worn-out by six and now slept through the night, waking to be fed around seven in the morning. Sheila couldn't help wondering if the baby's next caretaker would keep her on that same schedule.

She heard the doorbell ring as she moved down the stairs. She figured it was Summer dropping by to say hello, now that she'd dumped the flamingos off on someone's lawn. Quickly moving to the door so the sound of the bell wouldn't wake Sunnie, she glanced out the peephole and her heart thumped hard in her chest. It wasn't Summer. It was Zeke.

She didn't have to wonder why he'd dropped by. To spy on her and to make sure she was taking care of Sunnie properly. Drawing in a deep breath, she slowly opened the door.

Nine

She'd been crying. Zeke took note of that fact immediately. Her eyes were red and slightly puffy, and when he looked closer, he saw her chin was trembling as if she was fighting even now to keep tears at bay. He wasn't sure if the tears she was holding back were for Sunnie or what she assumed was his misuse of her.

He wanted more than anything to take her into his arms, pull her close and tell her how wrong she was and to explain how much she had come to mean to him. But he knew that he couldn't do that. Like him, his distrust of people's motives didn't start overnight. Therefore, he would have to back up anything he said. Prove it to her. Show her in deeds instead of just words. Eventually he'd have to prove every claim he would make here tonight.

He may have been the one abandoned as a child, but she, too, had been abandoned. Those who should have loved her, been there for her and supported her had not. In his book, that was the worse type of abandonment.

"Zeke, I know why you're here," she finally said, after they had stood there and stared at each other for a long moment.

"Do you?" he asked.

She lifted that trembling chin. "Yes. Sunnie's asleep. You're going to have to take my word for it, and we had a fun day. Now, goodbye."

She made an attempt to close the door, but he put his foot in the way. "Thanks for the information, but that's not why I'm here."

"Then why are you here?"

"To see the woman I made love to several times. The woman I had gotten used to waking up beside in the mornings. The woman I want even now."

She lifted her gaze from the booted foot blocking her door to him. "You shouldn't say things you don't mean."

"Sheila, we need to talk. I think I know what brought this on. I listened to the message my aunt left on my answering machine. You jumped to the wrong conclusion."

"Did I?"

"Yes, you did."

She crossed her arms over her chest. "I don't think so."

"But what if you did? Think of the huge mistake you're making. Invite me in and let's talk about it."

He watched as she began nibbling on her bottom lip, a lip he had sucked into his mouth, kissed and devoured many times since meeting her. Had it been less than two weeks? How had he fallen in love with her so quickly and know for sure it was the real thing?

He drew in a huge breath. Oh, it was definitely the real thing. Somehow, Sheila Hopkins had seeped into his bloodstream and was now making a huge statement within his heart.

"Okay, come in."

She stood back and he didn't waste any time entering in case she changed her mind. Once inside he glanced around the room and noticed how different things looked. All the baby stuff was gone. At least it had been collected and placed in a huge cardboard box that sat in the corner.

Not waiting for him to say anything when she saw the way his gaze had scanned the room, she said, "And please don't pretend that you don't know that I'll be turning Sunnie over to someone, as early as tomorrow."

He lifted a brow. "And someone told you that?"

She shrugged. "No, not really. But Ms. Talbert did call to say the results of the paternity test had come in. And since you were so certain Sunnie doesn't belong to your friend, then I can only assume that means she's going into the system."

He moved away from the door to walk over to stand in front of her. "You shouldn't assume anything. My investigation isn't over. And do you know what your problem is, Sheila?"

She stiffened her spine at his question. "What?"

"You assume too much and usually you assume wrong."

She glared at him before moving away to sit down on the sofa. "Okay, then you tell me, Zeke. How are my assumptions wrong?"

He dropped into the chair across from the sofa. "First of all, my aunt's phone call. She knew about the case I'm handling for Brad. And she knows Brad is my best friend and that I intend to clear his name or die trying. She was right. I intend to keep an eye on Sunnie and that might be the reason I hung around you at first. But that's not what brought me back here. If you recall, four days went by when I didn't see you or the baby."

"Then what brought you back?"

"You. I couldn't stay away from you."

He saw doubt in her eyes and knew he had his work cut out for him. But he would eventually make her believe him. He had to. Even now it was hard not to cross the room and touch her. Dressed in a pair of jeans and a pullover sweater and in bare feet, she looked good. Ravishing. Stunning. Even the puffiness beneath her eyes didn't take away her allure. And where she was sitting, the light from the fading sun made her skin glow, cast a radiant shine on her hair.

"Why didn't you tell me there was a chance the test results would come back early, to prepare me?"

"Because I know how attached you've gotten to Sunnie and I didn't want to deliver bad news any sooner than I had to. And what you assumed regarding that is wrong as well. The test results were not conclusive that Brad isn't Sunnie's father."

She leaned forward and narrowed her gaze accusingly. "But you were so convinced Bradford Price is not Sunnie's father."

"And I'm still convinced. The test reveals there is a genetic link. Now I'm going to find out how. It's not Brad's sister's child, but he did have a brother who died last year. I'd only met Michael once and that was when Brad and I were in college and he showed up asking Brad for money."

Zeke drew in a deep breath as he remembered that time. "Michael was his younger brother and, according to Brad, he got mixed up with the wrong crowd in high school, dropped out and became addicted to hard drugs. That's when Mr. Price disinherited him."

She nodded. "What happened to him?"

"Michael died in a drunk driving accident last year but foul play was never ruled out. There were some suspicious factors involved, including the amount of drugs they found in his system."

"That's horrible. But it would mean there was no way he could have fathered Sunnie."

"I thought about that possibility on the way here. He would have died a couple of months after she was conceived. It might be a long shot, but I am going to check it out. And Brad also has a few male cousins living in Waco. Like Brad, they enjoy their bachelor lifestyles, so I'll be checking with them as well."

She leaned back on the sofa. "So what will happen with Sunnie in the meantime?"

"That decision will be up to Social Services. However, I plan to have Brad recommend that she remain with you until this matter is resolved."

He saw the way her eyes brightened. "You think they'll go for it?"

"I don't know why they wouldn't. This is a delicate matter, and unfortunately it puts Brad in an awkward position. Even if Sunnie isn't directly his, there might be a family link. And knowing Brad the way I do, he will not turn his back on her, regardless. So either way, he might be filing for custody. She's doing fine right here with you, and the fewer changes we make with her the better."

He stood and crossed the room to sit beside her on the sofa. Surprised, she quickly scooted over. "Now that we got the issue of Sunnie taken care of, I think there is another matter we need to talk about," he said.

She nervously licked her lips. "And what issue is that?"

He stretched his arm across the back of the sofa. "Why you were so quick to assume the worst of me. Why you don't think I can care for you and refuse to believe that I'd want to develop a serious relationship with you."

"Why should I think you care and would want to develop something serious with me? No one else has before."

"I can't speak for those others, Sheila. I can only speak for myself."

"So you want me to believe it was more than just sex between us?" she asked stiffly.

"Yes, that's what I want you to believe."

It's a good thing he understood her not wanting to believe. How many times had he wanted to believe that if he got involved with someone seriously, they wouldn't just eventually disappear? And he knew deep down that's why he couldn't fully wrap his arms around the Travers family. A part of him was so afraid he would wake up one day and they would no longer want to include him in their lives. Although they had shown him more than once that was not the case, he still had those fears.

He stood and walked to the window and looked out. It was getting dark outside. He scrunched up his brow wondering why all those pink flamingos were across the street in Sheila's neighbor's yard and then remembered the TCC's fundraiser.

Drawing in a deep breath, he turned around to glance over at Sheila. She was watching him, probably wondering what he was about. What he had on his mind. "You know you aren't the only one who has reasons to want to be cautious about getting involved with someone. The main reason I shy away from any type of serious relationship is thinking the person will be here one day and gone the next."

At her confused expression he returned to sit beside her on the sofa. "My mother left me, literally gave me up to my aunt when I was only five. In other words, I was abandoned just like Sunnie. I didn't see her again until I turned nineteen. And that was only because she thought with my skills as a football player in college that I'd make the pros and would be her meal ticket."

He saw the pity that shone in Sheila's eyes. He didn't want her pity, just her understanding. "Since Mom left me, for a long time I thought if I did anything wrong my aunt would desert me as well."

"So you never did anything wrong."

"I tried not to. So you see, Sheila, I have my doubts about things just like you."

She didn't say anything for a moment and then asked, "What about your father?"

He leaned back on the sofa. "I never knew my father growing up. My aunt didn't have a clue as to his identity. My mother never told her. Then when I was in college, the craziest thing happened."

"What?" she asked, sitting up as if she was intrigued by what he was telling her.

"There was a guy on campus that everyone said looked just like me. I finally ran into him and I swear it was like looking in the mirror. He was younger than me by a year. And his name was Colin Travers."

"Your brother?"

"Yes, but we didn't know we were brothers because I was named Ezekiel Daniels at birth. Colin found our likeness so uncanny he immediately called his father. When he told his father my name, his old man remembered having a brief, meaningless affair with my mother years ago, before he married. He also remembered my mother's claim of getting pregnant when the affair ended. But she'd also made that claim to another man. So he assumed she was lying and had his attorney handle the situation. My mother wasn't absolutely sure Travers was my father, so she let it go."

"When your father finally discovered your existence, how did he treat you?" she asked.

"With open arms. All of his family welcomed me. His wife and my five brothers and one sister. At his request, on my twenty-first birthday, I changed my last name from Daniels to Travers and to this day that's all I've taken from him. And trust me he's offered plenty. But I don't take and I don't ask. Since acknowledging him as my father twelve years ago, I've never asked him for a single thing and I don't intend to."

"And who is your father, Zeke?"

"Matthew Travers."

Her mouth dropped open. "The self-made millionaire in Houston?"

He couldn't help chuckling at the shock he heard in her voice. "Yes. That's him."

"Do you blame him for not being a part of your life while growing up?"

"I did, but once I heard the whole story, and knowing my mother like I did, what he told me didn't surprise me. He felt badly about it and has tried making it up to me in various ways, although I've told him countless times that he doesn't owe me anything.

"So you see, Sheila, you aren't the only one with issues. I have them and I admit it. But I want to work on them with you. I want to take a chance and I want you to take a chance, too. What I feel with you feels right, and it has nothing to do with Sunnie."

He shook his head. "Hell, Sunnie's a whole other issue that I intend to solve. But I need to know that you're willing to step out on faith and give us a chance."

Sheila could feel a stirring deep in her heart. He was asking for them to have a relationship, something more than a tumble between the sheets. It was something she thought she'd had with Crawford, only to get hurt. Could she take a chance again?

"My last boyfriend was a medical-supply salesman. He traveled a lot, left me alone most of the time. I thought I'd be satisfied with his calls and always looked forward to his return. Then one day he came back just to let me know I'd gotten replaced."

"You don't need to worry about that happening," Zeke said quietly.

She glanced over at him. "And why wouldn't I?"

He leaned closer to her and said in a low husky tone, "Because I am so into you that I can't think straight. I go to sleep dreaming of you and I wake up wanting you. When I make love to you, I feel like I'm grabbing a piece of heaven."

"Oh, Zeke." She drew in a deep breath, thinking that if this was a game he was playing with her then he was playing it well. Stringing her as high and as tight as it could go. She wanted to believe it wasn't a game and that he was sincere. She so much wanted to believe.

"I will always be there for you, Sheila. Whenever you need me. I won't let you down. You're going to have to trust me. Believe in me."

She fought back the tears. "Please don't tell me those

things if you don't mean them," she said softly. "Please don't."

"I mean them and I will prove it," he said, reaching out and gently pulling her toward him.

"Just trust me," he whispered close to her lips. And then he leaned in closer and captured her mouth with his.

Sheila thought being in Zeke's arms felt right, so very right. And she wanted to believe everything he'd said, because as much as she had tried fighting it, she knew at that moment that she loved him. And his words had pretty much sealed her fate. Although he hadn't said he loved her, he wanted to be a part of her life and for them to take things one day at a time. That was more than anyone before had given her.

And she didn't have to worry about him being gone for long periods of time and not being there for her if she needed him.

But she didn't want to think about anything right now but the way he was kissing her. With a hunger she felt all the way to her bones.

And she was returning the kiss as heat was building inside her. Heat mixed with the love she felt for him. It was thrumming through her, stirring up emotions and feelings she'd tried to hold at bay for so long. But Zeke was pulling them out effortlessly, garnering her trust, making her believe and beckoning her to fall in love with him even more.

She felt herself being lifted into his arms and carried up the stairs. They didn't break mouth contact until he had lowered her onto the bed. "Mmm," she murmured in protest, missing the feel of his lips on hers, regretting the loss of tongue play in her mouth.

"I'm not going far, baby. We just need to remove our clothes," he whispered hotly against her moist lips.

Through desire-laden eyes she watched as he quickly removed his clothes and put on protection before returning to her. He reached out and took her hand and drew her closer to him. "Do you know how much I missed waking up beside you? Making love to you? Being inside you?"

She shook her head. "No."

"Then let me show you."

Zeke wanted to take things slow, refused to be rushed. He needed to make love to her the way he needed to breathe. After removing every stitch of her clothing, he breathed in her scent that he'd missed. "You smell good, baby."

"I smell like baby powder," she said, smiling. "One of the pitfalls of having a baby around."

His chuckle came out in a deep rumble. "You do smell like a baby. *My* baby." And then he kissed her again.

Moments later he released her mouth and began touching her all over as his hands became reacquainted with every part of her. He continued to stroke her and then his hands dipped to the area between her legs and found her wet and ready. Now another scent was replacing the baby powder fragrance and he was drawn into it. His erection thickened even more in response to it. He began stroking her there, fondling her, fingering the swollen bud of her womanhood.

"Zeke…"

"That's right, speak my name. Say it. I intend for it to be the only name you'll ever need to say when you feel this way."

And then he lowered himself to the bed, needing to

be inside her now. His body straddled hers and he met her gaze, held it, while slowly entering her. He couldn't help shuddering at the feel of the head of his shaft slowly easing through her feminine core.

She wrapped her legs around him and he began moving to a beat that had been instilled inside his head from the first time he'd made love to her. And he knew he would enjoy connecting with her this way until the day he took his last breath. He'd never desired a woman the way he desired her.

And then he began moving in and out of her. Thrusting deep, stroking long and making each one count. Shivers of ecstasy began running up his spine and he could feel his hardness swell even more inside her. He reached down, lifted her hips to go deeper still and it was then that she screamed his name.

His name.

And something exploded inside him, made him tremble while wrapped in tremendous pleasure. Made him utter her name in a guttural breath. And he knew at that moment, whatever it took, he was determined that one day she would love him back. He would prove to her she had become more than just temptation to him. She had become his life.

Sheila snuggled deeper into Zeke's arms and glanced over at the clock on her nightstand. It was almost midnight. They had gotten up earlier to check on Sunnie and to grab a light dinner—a snack was more like it. He had scrambled eggs and she had made hash browns. While they ate he told her more about his relationship with the Travers family. And she shared with him how awful things had been for her with Crawford, and how strained her relationships were with her mother and sister.

He had listened and then got up from the table to come around and wipe tears from her eyes before picking her up in his arms and taking her back upstairs where they had made love again. Now he was sleeping and she was awake, still basking in the afterglow of more orgasms tonight than she cared to count, but would always remember.

She gently traced the curve of his face with the tip of her finger. It was hard to believe this ultrahandsome man wanted her. He had a way of making her feel so special and so needed. Earlier tonight in this very bed she had felt so cold. But now she wasn't cold. Far from it. Zeke was certainly keeping her warm. She couldn't help smiling.

"Hmm, I hate to interrupt whatever it is you're thinking about that's making you smile, but…"

And then he reached up, hooked a hand behind her neck to bring her mouth down to his. And then he took possession of it in that leisurely but thorough way of his. And it was a way that had her toes tingling. Oh, Lord, the man could kiss. Boy, could he kiss. And to think she was the recipient of such a drugging connection.

He finally released her mouth and pulled her up to straddle him. He then gazed up at her as he planted his hands firmly on her hips. "Let's make love this way."

They had never made love using this position before, and she hesitated and just stared at him, not sure what he wanted her to do. He smiled and asked, "You can ride a horse, right?"

She nodded slowly. "Yes, of course."

"Then ride me."

She smiled as she lifted the lower part of her body and then came down on him. He entered her with accurate precision. She stifled a groan as he lifted his hips off the bed to go deeper inside her. She in turned pressed down as hard as she could, grinding her body against his.

And then she did what he told her to do. She rode him.

Brad glanced across the desk at Zeke. "Is there a reason you ran off yesterday like something was on fire?"

Zeke leaned back in his chair. He had left Sheila's house this morning later than he'd planned, knowing he had to go home first to change before heading into the office. He wasn't surprised to find Brad waiting on him. He'd seen the newspaper that morning. Brad's genetic connection to Sunnie made headline news, front page and center, for all to read.

When Zeke had stopped by the Royal Diner to grab a cup of coffee, the place where all the town gossips hung out, it seemed the place was all abuzz. There must have been a leak of information either at the lab where the test was processed or at the hospital. In any case, news of the results of the paternity test was all over town.

Everyone was shocked at the outcome of the test. Those who thought the baby wasn't Brad's due to the blackmailers hitting on other TCC members—even that news had somehow leaked—were going around scratching their heads, trying to figure out how the baby could be connected to Brad.

"It had to do with Sheila," he finally said.

Brad lifted a brow. "The woman taking care of the baby?"

"Yes."

Brad didn't say anything as he studied him, and Zeke knew exactly what he was doing. He was reading him like a book, and Zeke knew his best friend had the ability to do that. "And why do I get the feeling this Sheila Hopkins means something more to you than just a case you're working on?" Brad finally asked.

"Probably because you know me too well, and you're right. I met her less than two weeks ago and she has gotten to me, Brad. I think…I've fallen in love with her."

Zeke was certain Brad would have toppled over in his chair if it had not been firmly planted on the floor. "Love?"

"Yes, and I know what you're thinking. And it's not that. I care for her deeply." He leaned forward. "And she is even more cautious than I am about taking a chance. I'm the one who has to prove how much she means to me. Hell, I can't tell her how I feel yet. I'm going to have to show her."

A smile touched Brad's lips. "Well, this is certainly a surprise. I wish you the best."

"Thanks, man. And you might as well know one of her concerns right now is what's going to happen to Sunnie. She's gotten attached to her."

He paused a moment and then said, "Since you're here I have a video I want you to watch."

"A video?"

"Yes. I want you to look at that video I pulled that shows a woman placing the car seat containing the baby on the TCC doorstep. All we got is a good shot of her hands."

"And you think I might be able to recognize some woman's hands?" Brad asked.

Zeke shrugged. "Hey, it's worth a try." He picked up the remote to start rolling the videotape on the wide screen in his office.

Moments later they looked up when there was a tap

on the door. He then remembered his secretary had taken part of the morning off. "Come in."

Summer entered. "Hi, guys, sorry to interrupt. But you know it's fundraiser time for the shelter and I—"

She stopped talking when she glanced at the wide screen where Zeke had pressed Pause and the image had frozen on a pair of hands. "Why are you watching a video of Diane Worth's hands?"

Both men stared at her. Zeke asked in astonishment, "You recognize those hands?"

Summer smiled. "Yes, but only because of that tiny scar across the back of her right hand, which would have been a bigger scar if Dr. Harris hadn't sutured it the way he did. And then there's that little mole between the third and fourth finger that resembles a star."

Her smile widened when she added, "And before you ask, the reason I noticed so much about her hand is because I'm the one who bandaged the wound after Dr. Harris examined her."

Zeke got out of his chair to sit on the edge of his desk. "This woman came through the shelter recently?"

Summer shook her head. "Yes, around seven months ago. She was eight months pregnant and her boyfriend had gotten violent and cut her on her hand with a bowie knife. She wouldn't give the authorities his name, and stayed at the shelter one week before leaving without a trace in the middle of the night."

Zeke nodded slowly, not believing he might finally have a break in the case. "Do you have any information you can give us on her?"

"No, and by law our records are sealed to protect the women who come to the shelter for our protection. I can tell you, however, that the information she gave us wasn't correct. When she disappeared I tried to find

her to make sure she was okay and ran into a dead end.
I'm not even sure Diane Worth is her real name."

Zeke rubbed his chin. "And you said she was pregnant and vanished without a trace?"

"Yes, but Abigail might be able to help you further."

Brad lifted a brow. "Abigail Langley?"

Summer nodded. "Yes. It just so happened the night
Diane disappeared, we thought she might have met
with foul play. But Abigail had volunteered to man our
suicide phone line that night, and according to Abigail,
when she went out to put something in her car, she saw
Diane getting into a car with some man of her own free
will."

"That was a while back. I wonder if Abigail would
be able to identify the guy she saw?" Brad mused.

"We can pay Abigail a visit and find out," Zeke said.
He looked over at Summer. "We need a description of
Diane Worth for the authorities. Can we get it from
you?"

Summer smiled. "With a judge's order I can do better
than that. I can pull our security camera's tape of the
inside of the building. There were several in the lounge
area where Diane used to hang out. I bet we got some
pretty clear shots of her."

Adrenaline was flowing fast and furious through
Zeke's veins. "Where's Judge Meadows?" he asked Brad.

Brad smiled. "About to go hunting somewhere with
Dad. Getting that court order from him shouldn't be a
problem."

"Good," Zeke said, glancing down at his watch.
"First I want to pay Abigail Langley a visit. And then
I want to check out those videotapes from the shelter's
security camera."

"I'm coming with you when you question Abigail," Brad said, getting to his feet.

Zeke raised a brow. "Why?"

Brad shrugged. "Because I want to."

Zeke rolled his eyes as he moved toward the door. "Fine, but don't you dare make her cry again."

"You made Abigail cry?" Summer asked, frowning over at him.

"It wasn't intentional and I apologized," a remorseful-sounding Brad said, and he quickly followed Zeke out the door.

Ten

"You need a husband."

Sheila groaned inwardly. Her mother was definitely on a roll today. "No, I don't."

"Yes, you do, and with that kind of attitude you'll never get one. You need to return to Dallas and meet one of Charles's nephews."

Sheila shook her head. Her mother had called to brag about a new man she'd met. Some wealthy oilman and his two nephews. Cassie had warned her that they were short for Texans, less than six feet tall, but what they lacked in height, they made up for in greenbacks.

"So, will you fly up this weekend and—"

"No, Mom. I don't want to return to Dallas."

Her mother paused a moment and then said, "I wasn't going to mention it, but I ran into Crawford today."

Sheila drew in a deep breath. Hearing his name no longer caused her pain. "That's nice."

"He asked about you."

"I don't know why," she said, glancing across the room to where Sunnie was reaching for one of her toys.

"He's no longer with that woman and I think he wants you back," her mother said.

"I wouldn't take him back if he was the last man on earth."

"And you think you can be choosy?"

Sheila smiled, remembering that morning with Zeke. "Yes, I think I can."

"Well, I don't know who would put such foolishness into your head. I know men. They are what they are. Liars, cheaters, manipulators, all of them. The only way to stay ahead of them is to beat them at their own game. But don't waste your time on a poor one. Go after the ones with money. Make it worth your while."

A short time later as she gave Sunnie her bath, Sheila couldn't help thinking of what her mother said. That had always been her mother's problem. She thought life was a game. Get them before they get me first. There was no excuse for her cheating on her first husband. But then she had cheated on her second and fourth husbands, as well.

Her phone rang and she crossed the room to pick it up, hoping it wasn't her mother calling back with any more maternal advice. "Yes?"

"Hi, beautiful."

She smiled upon recognizing Zeke's voice. "Howdy, handsome."

She and Zeke had made love before he'd left that morning and she had felt tingly sensations running through her body all day. They had been a reminder of what the two of them had shared through the night.

And to think she had ridden him. Boy, had she ridden him. She blushed all over just thinking about it.

"I think we have a new lead," he said excitedly.

"You do? How?"

He told her how Summer had dropped by when he was showing the videotape in his office to Brad, and that she had identified the hands of the woman who had left Sunnie on the TCC's doorstep. He and Brad were now on their way to talk to Abigail Langley. There was a chance she could identify the man who the pregnant woman had left with that night. Then they would drop by the shelter to pull tapes for the authorities. There was a possibility Sunnie's mother was about to be identified.

By the time she'd hung up the phone from talking to Zeke, she knew he was closer to exposing the truth once and for all. Was Diane Worth Sunnie's biological mother? If she was, why did she leave her baby on the TCC's doorstep claiming she was Bradford Price's child?

Abigail led Zeke and Brad into the study of her home. "Yes, I can give you a description of the guy," she said, sitting down on a love seat. "I didn't know who he was then, but I do now from seeing a picture of him flash on television one night on CNN when they did an episode on drug rings in this country. His name is Miguel Rivera and he's reputed to be a drug lord with an organization in Denver."

"Denver?" Zeke asked, looking at Brad. "Why would a drug lord from Denver be in Royal seven months ago?"

Brad shrugged. "I wouldn't know unless he's connected to Paulo Rodriguez." Brad then brought Zeke up to date on what had gone on in Royal a few years ago when the local drug trafficker had entangled prominent TCC members in an embezzlement and arson scandal.

"I think I need to fly to Denver to see what I can find out," Zeke said. He glanced over at Abigail. "I appreciate you making time to see us today."

"I don't mind. No baby should have been abandoned like that."

Knowing that the subject of the baby was a teary subject with her for some reason, Zeke said, "Well, we'll be going. We need to stop by the shelter to see what we can find out there."

They were about to walk out the study, when Brad noticed something on the table and stopped. "You still have this?" he asked Abigail.

Zeke saw the trophy sitting on the table that had caught Brad's eye.

"Yes. I was cleaning out the attic at my parents' house and came across it," she said.

Intrigued, Zeke asked. "What is it for?"

"This," Brad said, chuckling as he picked up the trophy and held it up for Zeke to see, "should have been mine. Abigail and I were in a spelling bee. It was a contest that I should have won."

"But you didn't," she said, laughing. "I can't believe you haven't gotten over that. You didn't even know how to spell the word *occupation*."

"Hell, I tried," Brad said, joining her in laughter.

"Trying wasn't good enough that day, Brad. Get over it."

Zeke watched the two. It was evident they shared history. It was also evident they had always been rivals. He wondered if they could continue to take their boxing gloves off and share a laugh or two the way they were doing now more often.

After a few moments, the pair remembered he was there. Brad cleared his throat. "I guess we better get going to make it to the shelter. Goodbye, Abby."

"Bye, Brad, and I'll see you around, Zeke."

"Sure thing," Zeke responded, not missing the fact this was the second occasion that he'd heard Brad refer to her as Abby. The first time occurred when he'd been holding her in his arms, comforting her. Um, interesting.

"So what do you think?" Brad asked moments later while snapping on their seat belts in Zeke's car.

Zeke chuckled. "I think it's a damn shame you couldn't spell the word *occupation* and lost the spelling bee to a girl."

Brad threw his head back and laughed. "Hey, you didn't know Abigail back then. She was quite a pistol. She could do just about anything better than anyone."

Zeke wondered if Brad realized he'd just given the woman a compliment. "Evidently. Now to answer your question about Miguel Rivera, I think I'm going to have to fly to Denver. If Diane Worth is Sunnie's mother, I want to know what part Miguel Rivera is playing in her disappearance. I think all the answers lie in Denver."

Brad nodded. "And you think there's a possible connection to my brother, Michael?"

"I'm not sure. But I know that baby isn't yours and she has to belong to someone. And you and I know Michael was heavy into alcohol and drugs."

"Yes, but as a user, not a pusher," Brad said.

"As far as we know," Zeke countered. "When you went to collect his belongings, was there anything in them to suggest he might have been involved with a woman?"

"I wasn't checking for that. Besides, there wasn't much of anything in that rat hole he called an apartment.

I boxed up what he had, if you want to go through it. I put it in storage on my parents' property."

"I do. We can check that out after we leave the shelter." Zeke backed out of Abigail's driveway.

"You're leaving for Denver tomorrow?" Sheila asked hours later, glancing across the kitchen table at Zeke. He was holding Sunnie, making funny faces to get her to laugh. Sheila tried to downplay the feeling escalating inside her that he was leaving her.

This is work, you ninny, a voice inside her said. *This is not personal. He is not Crawford.* But then she couldn't help remembering Crawford's reason for leaving was all work-related, too.

"Yes, I need to check out this guy named Miguel Rivera. He might be the guy who picked Diane Worth up from the shelter that night. Thanks to security cameras inside the shelter, we were able to get such good shots of the woman that we've passed them on to law enforcement."

The woman who might be Sunnie's mother, she thought. "How long do you think you'll be gone?" she asked.

"Not sure. I don't intend to come back until I find out a few things. I have a lot of questions that need to be answered."

Sheila nodded. She knew his purpose in going to Denver would help close the case on Sunnie and bring closure. It was time, she knew that. But still… "Well, I hope you find out something conclusive. For Sunnie's sake," she said.

And for yours, Zeke thought, studying her features. He knew that with each day that passed, she was getting attached to Sunnie even more. The first thing he'd noticed when he arrived at her place was Sunnie's things were once again all over the place.

"So what are you going to be doing while I'm gone?" he asked her, standing to place the baby back in her seat.

"You can ask me that with Sunnie here? Trust me, there's never a dull moment." She paused and then asked quietly, "You won't forget I'm here, will you?"

He glanced up after snapping Sunnie into the seat. Although Sheila had tried making light of the question, he could tell from the look on her face she was dead serious. Did she honestly think when he left for Denver that he wouldn't think of her often, probably every single day? And although he would need to stay focused on solving the case, there was no doubt in his mind that she would still manage to creep into his thoughts. Mainly because she had his heart. Maybe it was time for him to tell her that.

He crossed the room to where she sat at the table and took her hands into his and eased her up. He then wrapped his arms around her waist. "There's no way I can forget about the woman I've fallen in love with."

He saw immediate disbelief flash across her features and said, "I know it's crazy considering we've only known each other for just two weeks but it's true. I do love you, Sheila, and no matter what you think, I won't forget you, and I am coming back. I will be here whenever you need me, just say the word."

He saw the tears that formed in her eyes and heard her broken words when she said, "And I love you, too. But I'm scared."

"And you think I'm not scared, too, baby? I've never given a woman my heart before. But you have it—lock, stock and barrel. And I don't make promises I don't keep, sweetheart. I will always be here for you. I will be a man you can count on."

And then he lowered his mouth and sealed his promise with a kiss, communicating with her this way and letting her know what he'd just said was true. He wanted her, but he loved her, too.

She returned his kiss with just as much fervor as he was putting into it. He knew if they didn't stop he would be tempted to haul her upstairs, which couldn't happen since Sunnie was wide awake. But there would be later and he was going to start counting the minutes.

Sheila woke when the sunlight streaming through the window hit her in the face. She jerked up in bed and saw the side next to her was empty. Had Zeke left for Denver already without telling her goodbye?

Trying to ignore the pain settling around her heart, she wrapped the top sheet around her naked body and eased out of bed to stare out the window. Was he somewhere in the skies on a plane? He hadn't said when he was returning, but he said he would and that he loved her. He *loved* her. She wanted so much to believe him and—

"Is there any reason you're standing there staring out the window?"

She whipped around with surprise all over her face. "You're here."

He chuckled. "Yes, I'm here. Where did you think I'd be?"

She shrugged. "I assumed you had left for Denver already."

"Without telling you goodbye?"

She fought back telling him that's how Crawford would do things, and that he had a habit of not returning when he'd told her he would. Something would always come up. There was always that one last sale he just had to make. Instead, she said, "What you have to do in Denver is important."

He leaned in the doorway with a cup of coffee in his hand. "And so are you."

He entered the room and placed the cup on the nightstand. "Come here, sweetheart."

She moved around the bed, tugging the sheet with her. When she came to a stop in front of him, he said, "Last night I told you that I had fallen in love with you, didn't I?"

"Yes."

"Then I need for you to believe in me. Trust me. I know, given your history with the people you care about, trusting might not be easy, but you're going to have to give me a chance."

She drew in a deep breath. "I know, but—"

"No buts, Sheila. We're in this thing together, you and me. We're going to leave all our garbage at the back door and not bring it inside. All right?"

She smiled and nodded. "All right."

He was about to pull her into his arms, when they heard the sound of Sunnie waking up on the monitor in the room. "I guess we'll have to postpone this for later. And later sometime, I need to look through some boxes Brad put in storage that belonged to his brother. His cousins in Waco swear they are not Sunnie's daddy, and since Michael is not here to speak for himself, I need to do some digging. But I am flying out for Denver tomorrow sometime."

He took a step back. "You go get dressed. Take your time. I'll handle the baby. And please don't ask if I know how to dress and feed her. If you recall, I've done it before."

She chuckled. "I know you have. And you will make a great father."

His smile widened. "You think so?"

"Yes."

"I take that as a compliment," he said. "And like I said, take your time coming downstairs. Sunnie and I will be in the kitchen waiting whenever you come down."

Zeke decided to do more than just dress and feed Sunnie. By the time Sheila walked into the kitchen, looking as beautiful as ever in black slacks and a pretty pink blouse, he had a suggestion for her. "The weather is nice outside. How about if we do something?"

She raised a brow. "Do something like what?"

"Um, like taking Sunnie to that carnival over in Somerset."

"But I thought you had to go through Brad's brother's boxes," she said.

"I do, but I thought we could go to the carnival first and I can look through the boxes later. I just called the airlines. I'll be flying out first thing in the morning, and I want to spend as much time as I can today with my two favorite ladies."

"Really?"

He could tell by her expression that she was excited by his suggestion. "Yes, really. What do you say?"

She practically beamed. "Sunnie and I would love to go to the carnival with you."

Considering how many items they had to get together for Sunnie, it didn't take long for them to be on their way. He had passed the carnival a few days ago and had known he wanted to take Sheila and Sunnie there. It had been only a couple of weeks, but Sunnie had become just as much a part of his life as Sheila's.

Although he'd told her how he felt about her, he could see Sheila was still handling him with caution, as if she was afraid to give her heart to him no matter how much she wanted to. He would be patient and continue to show her how much she meant to him. As he'd told her, considering her mother, sister and ex-boyfriend's treatment of her, he could definitely understand her lack of trust.

"And you're sure Brad is okay with you putting the investigation on hold to spend time with me and Sunnie?"

He glanced over at her as he turned toward the interstate. "Positive. A few hours won't hurt anything. Besides, I'll probably be gone most of next week and I'm missing you already."

It didn't take them long to reach the carnival grounds. After putting Sunnie in her stroller, they began walking around. It was Saturday and a number of people were out and about. He recognized a number of them he knew and Sheila ran into people she knew, as well. They ran into Brad's sister, Sadie, her husband, Ron, and the couple's twin daughters.

"She is a beautiful baby," Sadie said, hunching down to be eye level with Sunnie.

And as usual when strangers got close, Sunnie glanced around to make sure Sheila was near. "Yes, she is," Sheila said, smiling. She waited to see if the woman would make a comment about Sunnie favoring her brother or anyone in the Price family, but Sadie Price Pruitt didn't do so. But it was plain to see she was just as taken with Sunnie as Sheila was with Sadie's twins.

They also ran into Mitch Hayward and the former Jenny Watson. Mitch was the interim president of the TCC, and Jenny, one of his employees, when the two had fallen in love. And they had a baby on the way.

But the person Zeke was really surprised to see was Darius. He hadn't known his partner had returned to town. "Darius, when did you get back?" he asked, shaking his business partner's hand.

"Last night. We finished up a few days early and I caught the first plane coming this way."

Zeke didn't have to ask why when Darius drew Summer closer to him and smiled down at her.

"I would have called when I got in, but it was late and…"

Zeke chuckled. "Hey, man, you don't have to explain. I understand." He was about to introduce Darius and Sheila, but realized when Darius reached out and gave Sheila a hug that they already knew each other.

"And this is the little lady I've heard so much about," Darius said, smiling at Sunnie. "She's a beautiful baby."

They all chatted for few minutes longer before parting ways, but not before agreeing to get together when Zeke returned from Denver.

"I like Darius and Summer," Sheila said. "That time when Summer and I worked together on that abuse case, Darius was so supportive and it's evident that he loves her very much."

Zeke nodded and thought that one day he and Sheila might share the kind of bond that Darius and Summer enjoyed.

Eleven

Zeke was grateful for the friendships he'd made while at UT on the football team. The man he needed to talk to who headed Denver's Drug Enforcement Unit, Harold Mathis, just so happened to be the brother of one of Zeke's former teammates.

Mathis wasted no time in telling Zeke about Miguel Rivera. Although the notorious drug lord had been keeping a low profile lately, in no way did the authorities believe he had turned over a new leaf. And when they were shown photographs of Diane Worth, they identified her as a woman who'd been seen with Rivera once or twice.

Zeke knew he had his work cut out in trying to make a connection between Diane Worth and Michael Price. Michael's last place of residence was in New Orleans. At least that's where Brad had gone to claim his brother's body.

His belongings hadn't given a clue as to who he might have associated with, especially a woman by the name of Diane Worth. But Zeke was determined to find out if Diane Worth was Sunnie's mother.

The Denver Drug Enforcement Unit was ready to lend their services to do anything they could to get the likes of Miguel Rivera off the streets. So far he had been wily where the authorities were concerned and had been able to elude all undercover operations to nab him.

Since Zeke knew he would probably be in Denver awhile, he had decided to take residence in one of those short-term executive apartments. It wasn't home, but it had all the amenities. He had stopped by a grocery store to buy a few things and was reminded of the time when he had gone grocery shopping with Sheila and the baby when they'd stayed over at his place. He had been comfortable walking beside her and hadn't minded when a few people saw them and probably thought they were an item. As far as he was concerned, they were.

He glanced out a window that had a beautiful view of downtown Denver. He was missing his *ladies* already. Sunnie had started to grow on him as well, which was easy for her because she was such a sweet baby. She no longer screamed around strangers, although you could tell she was most comfortable when he or Sheila was around.

Sheila.

God, he loved her something awful and was determined that distance didn't put any foolishness in her mind, like her thinking he was falling out of love with her just because he didn't see her every day. Already he'd patronized the florist shop next door. They would make sure a bouquet of flowers was delivered to

Sheila every few days. And he intended to ply her with "thinking of you" gifts often.

He chuckled. Hell, that could get expensive because he thought of her all the time. The only time he would force thoughts of her from his mind was when he was trying to concentrate on the case. And even then it was hard.

He picked up the documents he had tossed on the table that included photographs of both Rivera and Worth. A contact was working with hospitals in both New Orleans and Denver to determine if a child was born to Diane Worth five months ago. And if so, where was the baby now?

He was about to go take a shower, when his phone rang. "Hello."

"I got another blackmail letter today, Zeke."

He nodded. Zeke figured another one would be coming sooner or later. The extortionist had made good his threat. But that didn't mean he was letting Brad off the hook. It was done mainly to let him know he meant business. "He still wants money, right?"

"Yes, and unless I pay up, Sunnie's birth records will be made public to show I had a relationship with a prostitute."

Of course, that was a lie, but the blackmailer's aim was to get money out of Brad to keep a scandal from erupting. It would have a far-reaching effect not only for Brad's reputation but that of his family.

"I know it's going to be hard for you to do, but just ignore it for now. Whoever is behind the extortion attempt evidently thinks he has you where he wants you to be, and we're going to prove him wrong."

By the time Zeke ended his call with Brad, he was more determined than ever to find a link between Rivera and Worth.

* * *

"You're thinking about getting married?" *Again?* Sheila really should not be surprised. Her mother hated being single and had a knack for getting a husband whenever she wanted one...

"Um, I'm thinking about it. I really like Charles."

You only met him last week. And wasn't it just a couple of weeks ago she'd asked her about Dr. Morgan? Sheila decided not to remind her mother of all those other men she'd liked, as well. "I wish you the best, Mom." And she did. She wanted her mother to be happy. Married or not.

"Thanks. And what's that I hear in the background? Sounds like a kid."

Sheila had no intention of telling her mother the entire story about Sunnie. "It is a baby. I'm taking care of her for a little while." That wasn't totally untrue since she was considered Sunnie's caretaker for the time being.

"That's nice, dear, since chances are you won't have any of your own. Your biological clock is ticking and you have no prospects."

Sheila smiled, deciding to let her mother think whatever she wanted. "You don't have to have a man to get pregnant, Mom. Just sperm."

"Please don't do anything foolish. I hope you aren't thinking of going that route. Besides, being pregnant can mess up a woman's figure for life."

Sheila rolled her eyes. Her mother thought nothing of blaming her for the one stretch mark she still had on her tummy. She was about to open her mouth and say something—to change the subject—when her doorbell sounded.

"Mom, I have to go. There's someone at the door."

"Be careful. There are lunatics living in small towns."

"Okay, Mom, I'll be careful." At times it was best not to argue.

After hanging up the phone, she glanced over at Sunnie, who was busy laughing while reaching for a toy that let out a squeal each time Sunnie touched it. She was such a happy baby.

Sheila glanced through the peephole. There was a woman standing there holding an arrangement of beautiful flowers. Sheila immediately figured the delivery was for her neighbor, who probably wasn't at home. She opened the door. "Yes, may I help you?"

The woman smiled. "Yes, I have a delivery for Sheila Hopkins."

Sheila stared at the woman, shocked. "I'm Sheila Hopkins. Those are for me?"

"Yes." The woman handed her a huge arrangement in a beautiful vase. "Enjoy them."

The woman then left, leaving Sheila standing there, holding the flowers with the shocked look still in place. It took the woman driving off before Sheila pulled herself together to take a step back into the house and close the door behind her as she gazed at the flowers. It was a beautiful bouquet. She quickly placed the vase in what she considered the perfect spot before pulling off the card.

I am thinking of you. Zeke.

Sheila's heart began to swell. He was away but still had her in his thoughts. A feeling of happiness spread through her. Zeke, who claimed he loved her, was too real to be true. She wanted to believe he was real...but...

She turned to Sunnie. "Look what Zeke sent. I feel special...and loved."

Sunnie didn't pay her any attention as she continued

to play with the toy Zeke had won for her at the carnival. Sheila was satisfied that even if Sunnie wasn't listening, her heart was. Now, if she could just shrug off her inner fear that regardless of what he did or said, for her Zeke was a heartbreak waiting to happen.

A few days later, during a telephone conversation with a Denver detective, Zeke's hand tightened on the phone. "Are you sure?" he asked.

"Yes," the man replied. "I verified with a hospital in New Orleans that Diane Worth gave birth to a baby girl there five months ago. We could pick her up for questioning since abandoning a baby is a punishable crime."

Zeke inhaled a deep breath. "She could say the baby is living somewhere with relatives or friends, literally having us going around in circles. We need proof she's Sunnie's mother and have that proof when she's brought in. Otherwise, she'll give Miguel Rivera time to cover his tracks."

Zeke paused a moment and then added, "We need a DNA sample from Worth. How can we get it without her knowing about it?"

"I might have an idea." The agent then shared his idea with Zeke.

Zeke smiled. "That might work. We need to run it by Mathis."

"It's worth a try if it will link her to Rivera. We want him off the streets and behind bars as soon as possible. He's bad news."

Later that night, as he did every night, Zeke called Sheila. Another bouquet of flowers as well as a basket of candy had been delivered that day. He had been plying her with "thinking of you" gifts since he'd been gone, trying to keep her thoughts on him and to let her know how much he was missing her.

After thanking him for her gifts, she mentioned that Brad had stopped by to see how Sunnie was doing. Sheila had been surprised to see him, but was glad he had cared enough about the baby's welfare to make an unexpected visit. She even told Zeke how Sunnie had gone straight to the man without even a sniffle. And that she seemed as fascinated with him as he had been with her.

Zeke then brought her up to date on what they'd found out about Diane Worth. "It seems she has this weekly appointment at a hair salon. One of the detectives will get hair samples for DNA testing. Once they have a positive link to Sunnie, they will bring her in for questioning."

"What do you think her connection is to Michael Price?" Sheila asked.

"Don't know for sure, but I have a feeling things will begin to unravel in a few more days."

They talked a little while longer. He enjoyed her sharing Sunnie's activities for that day, especially how attached she had gotten to that toy he'd won for her at the carnival.

"I miss you," he said, meaning it. He hadn't seen her in over a week.

"And I miss you, too, Zeke."

He smiled. That's what he wanted to hear. And since they were on a roll… "And I love you," he added.

"And I love you back. Hurry home."

Home. His chest swelled with even more love for her at that moment. "I will, just as soon as I get this case solved." And he meant it.

* * *

A few days later things began falling into place. As usual, Worth had her hair appointment. It took a couple of days for the DNA to be matched with the sample taken from Sunnie. The results showed Diane was definitely Sunnie's biological mother.

Although Zeke wasn't in the interrogation room when Worth was brought in, she did what they assumed she would do—denying the abandoned child could be hers. She claimed her baby was on a long trip with her father. However, once proof was presented showing Sunnie was her child and had been used in a blackmail scheme, and that her hand had been caught on tape, which could be proven, the woman broke down and blurted out what she knew of the sordid scheme.

She admitted that Rivera had planned for her to meet Michael Price for the sole purpose of having him get her pregnant. Once Rivera found out Michael was from a wealthy family, he set up his plan of extortion. She was given a huge sum of money to seduce Michael, and once her pregnancy was confirmed, Rivera had shown up one night and joined the party. Throughout the evening at Diane's, he'd spiked Michael's drinks with a near-lethal dose of narcotics and made sure he got behind the wheel to drive home. What had been made to look like a drunk-driving accident was anything but—Michael had been murdered. She also said that up until that night, Michael had been drug-free for almost six months and had intended to reunite with his family and try to live a decent life. With Worth's confession linking Rivera to Michael's death, a warrant was issued and Rivera was arrested.

Zeke had kept Brad informed of what was going on. The Price family was devastated to learn the truth behind Michael's death and looked forward to making Sunnie part of their family. Brad, who had never given up hope that Michael would have eventually gotten his life together if he'd survived, had decided to be Sunnie's legal guardian. He felt Michael would have wanted things that way.

That night when he called Sheila and heard the excitement in her voice about receiving candy and more flowers he'd sent, he hated to be the deliverer of what he had to tell her. Although it was good news for Sunnie, because she would he raised by Brad and kept out of the system, it would be a sad time for Sheila.

"The flowers are beautiful, Zeke, and the candy was delicious. If I gain any weight it will be your fault."

He smiled briefly and then he said in a serious tone, "We wrapped things up today, Sheila. Diane Worth confessed and implicated Miguel Rivera in the process. He then told her how things went down and how in the end the authorities had booked both Worth and Rivera. Since Worth worked with the authorities, she would get a lighter sentence, and Rivera was booked for the murder of Michael Price.

"That is so sad, but at least we know what happened and why Brad had a genetic link to Sunnie," she said softly.

"Yes, and Brad is stepping up to the plate to become Sunnie's legal guardian. He's going to do right by her. Already his attorneys have filed custody papers and there is no doubt in my mind he will get it. That's another thing Worth agreed to do to get a lighter sentence. She will give up full rights to Sunnie. She didn't deserve her anyway. She deliberately got pregnant to use her baby to get money."

Zeke paused and then added, "She claims she didn't

know of Rivera's plans to kill Michael until it was too late."

"I guess that means I need to begin packing up Sunnie's stuff. He'll come and get her any day," Sheila said somberly.

"According to Brad, Social Services told him the exchange needs to take place at the end of the week. I'll be back by then. I won't let you be alone."

He thought he heard her sniffing before she said, "Thanks, Zeke. It would mean a lot to me if you were here."

They talked for a little while longer before saying good-night and hanging up the phone. Zeke could tell Sheila was sad at the thought of having to give up Sunnie and wished he was there right now to hold her in his arms, make love to her and assure her everything would be all right. They would have babies of their own one day. All the babies she could ever want, and that was a promise he intended to make to her when he saw her again.

A couple of days later, after putting Sunnie down after her breakfast feeding, Sheila's phone rang. "Hello?"

"Sheila, this is Lois. Are you okay?"

Sheila almost dropped the phone. The last time her sister called her was to cancel her visit to see her and her family. "Yes, why wouldn't I be?"

"You were mentioned on the national news again. The Denver police and some hotshot private investigator solved this murder case about a drug lord. According to the news, he'd been using women to seduce rich men, get pregnant by them and then use the resulting babies as leverage for extortion. I understand such a thing happened in Royal and you are the one taking care of the abandoned baby while the case was being solved."

Sheila released a disappointed sigh. Ever since the story had broken, several members of the media had contacted her for a story and she'd refused to give them one. Why did her sister only want to connect with her when she appeared in the news or something? "Yes, that's true."

"That's wonderful. Well, Ted was wondering if perhaps you could get in touch with the private investigator who helped to solve the case."

"Why?"

"To have him on his television talk show, of course. Ted's ratings have been down recently and he thinks the man's appearance will boost them back up."

Sheila shook her head. Not surprising that Lois wanted something of her. Why couldn't she call just because?

"So, do you have a way to help Ted get in touch with his guy?" Lois asked, interrupting Sheila's thoughts.

"Yes, in fact I know him very well. But if you or Ted want to contact him you need to do it without my help," she said. "I'm your sister and the only time you seem to remember that is when you need a favor. That's not the kind of relationship I want with you, Lois, and if that's the only kind you're willing to give then I'm going to pass. Goodbye."

She hung up the phone and wasn't surprised when Lois didn't call back. And she wasn't surprised when she received a call an hour later from her mother.

"Really, Sheila, why do you continue to get yourself in these kinds of predicaments? You know nothing about caring for a baby. How did you let yourself be talked into being any child's foster parent?"

Sheila rolled her eyes. "I'm a nurse, Mom. I'm used to taking care of people."

"But a kid? Better you than me."

"How well I know that," she almost snapped

Her mother's comments reminded her that in two days she would hand Sunnie over to Bradford Price. He had called last night and they had agreed the exchange would take place at the TCC. It seemed fitting since that was the place Diane Worth had left her daughter— although for all the wrong reasons—that she would begin her new life there again.

Sheila wasn't looking forward to giving up Sunnie. The only good thing was that Zeke would be flying in tonight and she wouldn't be alone. He would give her his support. No one had ever done that for her before. And she couldn't wait to see him again after almost two weeks.

Zeke paused in the middle of packing for his return home and met DEA Agent Mathis's intense gaze. "What do you mean Rivera's attorney is trying to get him off on a technicality? We have a confession from Diane Worth."

"I know," Mathis said in a frustrated tone, "but Rivera has one of the slickest lawyers around. They are trying to paint Worth as a crackhead and an unfit mother who'd desert her child for more drugs, and that she thought up the entire thing—the murder scheme— on her own. The attorney is claiming his client is a model citizen who is being set up."

"That's bull and you and I know it."

"Yes, and since he drove from Denver to New Orleans instead of taking a flight, we can't trace the car he used." Mathis let out a frustrated sigh and added,

"This is what we've been dealing with when it comes to Rivera. He has unscrupulous people on his payroll. He claims he was nowhere near New Orleans during the time Michael Price was killed. We have less than twenty-four hours to prove otherwise or he walks."

"Damn." Zeke rubbed his hand down his face. "I refuse to let him get away with this. I want to talk to Worth again. There might be something we missed that can prove that now she's the one being set up."

A few hours later Zeke and Mathis were sitting at a table across from Diane Worth. "I don't care what Miguel is saying," she said almost in tears. "He is the one who came up with the plan, not me."

"Is there any way you can prove that?" Zeke asked her. He glanced at his watch. He should be on a plane right this minute heading for Royal. Now he would have to call Sheila to let her know he wouldn't be arriving in Royal tonight as planned. He refused to leave Denver knowing there was a chance Miguel Rivera would get away with murder.

She shook her head. "No, there's no way I can prove it." And then she blinked as if she remembered something. "Wait a minute. When we got to New Orleans we stopped for gas and Miguel went inside to purchase a pack of cigarettes. The store clerk was out of his brand and he pitched a fit. Several people were inside the store and I bet one of them remembers him. He got pretty ugly."

Zeke looked over at Mathis. "And even if they don't remember him, chances are, the store had a security camera."

Both men quickly stood. They had less than twenty-four hours to prove Miguel was in New Orleans when he claimed that he wasn't.

* * *

Sheila shifted in bed and glanced over at the clock as excitement flowed down her spine. Zeke's plane should have landed by now. He would likely come straight to her place from the airport. At least he had given her the impression that he would when she'd talked to him that morning. And she couldn't wait to see him.

She had talked to Brad and she would deliver Sunnie to him at the TCC at three the day after tomorrow. It was as if Sunnie had detected something was bothering her and had been clingy today. Sheila hadn't minded. She had wanted to cling to the baby as much as Sunnie had wanted to cling to her.

She smiled when her cell phone rang. She picked it up and checked caller ID. It was Zeke. She sat up in bed as she answered it. "Are you calling to tell me you're outside?" she asked, unable to downplay the anticipation as well as the excitement in her voice.

"No, baby. I'm still in Denver. Something came up with the case and I won't be returning for possibly three days."

Three days? That meant he wouldn't be there when she handed Sunnie over to Bradford Price. "But I thought you were going to return tonight so you could be here on Thursday. For me."

"I want to and will try to make it, but—"

"Yes, I know. Something came up. I understand," she said, trying to keep the disappointment out of her voice. Why had she thought he was going to be different?

"I've got to go, Zeke."

"No, you don't. You're shutting me out, Sheila. You act as if I'd rather be here than there, and that's not true and you know it."

"Do I?"

"You should. I need to be here or else Miguel Rivera gets to walk away scot-free."

A part of her knew she was being unreasonable. He had a job to do. But still, another part just couldn't accept he wasn't doing a snow job on her. "And of course you can't let him do that," she said snippily.

He didn't say anything for a minute and then, "You know what your problem is, Sheila? You can't take hold of the future because you refuse to let go of the past. Think about that and I'll see you soon. Goodbye."

Instead of saying goodbye, she hung up the phone. How dare he insinuate she was the one with the problem? What made him think that he didn't have issues? She didn't know a single person who didn't.

She shifted back down in bed, refusing to let Zeke's comments get to her. But she knew it was too late. They already had.

Twelve

Two days later, it was a tired Zeke who made it to the Denver airport to return to Royal. He and Mathis had caught a flight from Denver to New Orleans and interviewed the owner of the convenience store. The man's eyewitness testimony, as well as the store's security camera, had pinned Rivera in New Orleans when he said he hadn't been there. With evidence in hand, they had left New Orleans to return to Denver late last night.

After reviewing the evidence this morning, a judge had ruled in their favor and had denied bail to Rivera and had refused to drop the charges. And if that wasn't bad enough, the lab had delivered the results of their findings. DNA of hair found on Michael's jacket belonged to Rivera. Zeke was satisfied that Rivera would be getting just what he deserved.

He glanced at his watch. The good thing was that he was returning to Royal in two days instead of three. It wasn't noon yet and if his flight left on time, he would arrive back in Royal around two, just in time to be with Sheila when she handed Sunnie over to Brad. He had called her that morning from the courthouse in Denver and wasn't sure if she had missed his call or deliberately not answered it. He figured she was upset, but at some point she had to begin believing in him. If for one minute she thought she was getting rid of him she had another thought coming. She was his life and he intended to be hers.

A few moments later he checked his watch again thinking they should be boarding his plane any minute. He couldn't wait to get to Royal and see Sheila to hold her in his arms, make love to her all night. He hadn't meant to fall in love with her.

An announcement was made on the nearby intercom system, interrupting his thoughts. *"For those waiting on Flight 2221, we regret to inform you there are mechanical problems. Our take-off time has been pushed back three hours."*

"Damn." Zeke said, drawing in a frustrated breath. He didn't have three hours. He had told Sheila he was going to try to be there, and he intended to do just that. She needed him today and he wanted to be there for her. He could not and would not let her down.

He knew the only way he could make that happen. He pulled his phone out of his pocket and punched in a few numbers.

"Hello?"

He swallowed deeply before saying, "Dad, this is Zeke."

There was a pause and then, "Yes, son?"

Zeke drew in another deep breath. He'd never asked his father for anything, but he was doing so now. "I have a favor to ask of you."

* * *

"Thank you for taking care of her, Ms. Hopkins," Bradford Price said as Sheila handed Sunnie over to him the next day at the TCC headquarters.

"You don't have to thank me, Mr. Price. It's been a joy taking care of Sunnie these past few weeks," Sheila said, fighting back her tears. "And I have all her belongings packed and ready to be picked up. You paid for all of it and you'll need every last item." Sunnie was looking at her, and Sheila refused to make eye contact with the baby for fear she would lose it.

"All right. I'm make arrangements to drop by your place sometime later, if that's all right," Brad said.

"Yes, that will be fine." She then went down a list of dos and don'ts for the baby, almost choking on every word. "She'll be fussy if she doesn't eat breakfast by eight, and she sleeps all through the night after being given a nice bath. Seven o'clock is her usual bedtime. She takes a short nap during the day right after her lunch. She has a favorite toy. It's the one Zeke won for her at the carnival. She likes playing with it and will do so for hours."

"Thanks for telling me all that, and if it makes you feel better to know although I'm a bachelor, I plan to take very good care of my niece. And I know a little about babies myself. My sister has twin girls and I was around them a lot when they were babies."

"Sorry, Mr. Price, I wasn't trying to insinuate you wouldn't take good care of her."

Bradford Price smiled. "I know. You love her. I could see it in your eyes when you look at her. And please call me Brad. Mr. Price is my father."

A pain settled around Sheila's heart when she remembered Zeke's similar comment. Then later, he had explained why he'd said it. She was missing him so much and knew she hadn't been fair to him when he'd called last night to explain his delay in returning to Royal.

"Yes, I love her, Brad. She's an easy baby to love. You'll see." She studied him a minute. He was Zeke's best friend. She wondered how much he knew about their relationship. At the moment it didn't matter what he knew or didn't know. He was going to be Sunnie's guardian and she believed in her heart he would do right by his niece.

"I'm looking forward to making her an integral part of my family. Michael would have wanted it that way. I loved my brother and all of us tried reaching out to help him. It was good to hear he was trying to turn his life around, and a part of me believes that eventually he would have. It wasn't fair the way Miguel Rivera ended his life that way."

"No, it wasn't," she agreed.

"That's why Zeke remained in Denver a couple more days," Brad said. "Rivera's shifty attorney tried to have the charges dropped, claiming Rivera wasn't in New Orleans when Michael died. Zeke and the DEA agent had to fly to New Orleans yesterday to get evidence to the contrary. Now Rivera will pay for what he did. And I got a call from Zeke an hour ago. His flight home has been delayed due to mechanical problems."

Sheila nodded. Now she knew why Zeke wasn't there. She understood. She should have understood two nights ago, but she hadn't given him the chance to explain. Now, not only was she losing Sunnie, she had lost Zeke, as well.

She'd pushed him away because she couldn't let go of the past. She was so afraid of being abandoned;

she couldn't truly open her heart to him. And now she feared she was truly alone.

She continued to fight back her tears. "I call her Sunnie," she said, fighting to keep her voice from breaking. "But I'm sure you're going to name her something else."

Brad smiled as he looked at the baby he held. "No, Sunnie is her name and it won't get changed. I think Sunnie Price fits her." He then glanced over at her. "What's your middle name?"

She was surprised by his question. "Nicole."

"Nice name. How does Sunnie Nicole Price sound?"

Sheila could barely find her voice to ask. "You'll name her after me?"

Brad chuckled. "Yes, you took very good care of her and I appreciate it. Besides, you're her godmother."

That came as another surprise. "I am?"

"I'd like you to be. I want you to always be a part of my niece's life, Sheila."

Joy beamed up inside Sheila. "Yes, yes, I'd love to. I would be honored."

"Good. I'll let you know when the ceremony at the church will be held."

"All right."

"Now I better get her home."

Sheila leaned up and kissed Sunnie on the cheek. The baby had taken to Brad as easily as she had taken to her and that was a good sign. "You better behave, my sunshine." And before she could break down then and there, she turned and quickly walked away.

Sheila made it to the nearest ladies' room and it was there that the tears she couldn't hold back any longer came flooding through and she began crying in earnest. She cried for the baby she'd just given up and for the man she had lost. She was alone, but being alone was the story of her life, and it shouldn't have to be this way. She wanted her own baby one day, just like Sunnie, but she knew that would never happen. She would never find a man to love her again. A man who'd want to give her his babies. She'd had such a man and now he probably didn't want to see her again. He was right. She couldn't take hold of the future because she refused to let go of the past.

She saw that now. Zeke was right. It was her problem. But he wasn't here for her to tell that to. He had no reason to want to come back to her. She was a woman with issues and problems.

"Excuse me. I don't want to intrude, but are you all right?"

Sheila turned at the sound of the feminine voice and looked at the woman with the long, wavy red hair and kind blue eyes. She was a stranger, but for some reason the woman's question opened the floodgates even more and Sheila found herself crying out her pain, telling the woman about Sunnie, about the man she loved and had lost, and how she'd also lost the chance to ever have a child of her own.

The stranger gave her a shoulder to cry on and provided her with comfort when she needed it. "I understand how you feel. More than anything I'd love to have a child, but I can't have one of my own," the woman said, fighting back her own tears.

"My problem is physical," she continued as a slow trickle of tears flowed down her cheeks. "Every time I think I've accepted the doctor's prognosis, I discover I truly haven't, so I know just how you feel. I want a child so badly and knowing I can't ever have one is something I've yet to accept, although I know I must."

Sheila began comforting the woman who just a moment ago had comforted her.

"By the way, I don't think I've introduced myself. I'm Abigail Langley," the woman said once she'd calmed down.

"I'm Sheila Hopkins." She felt an affinity for the woman, a special bond. Although they had just met, she had a feeling this would be the start of an extraordinary friendship. She was convinced she and Abigail would be friends for life.

A short while later they managed to pull themselves together and with red eyes and swollen noses they walked out of the ladies' room, making plans to get together for lunch one day soon.

The sun was shining bright when Sheila and Abigail stepped outside. Sheila glanced up into the sky. Although it was a little on the chilly side, it was a beautiful day in November. The sun was shining and it made her think of Sunnie. Thanksgiving would be next week and she had a feeling Brad would have a big feast to introduce the baby to his entire family.

Abigail nudged her in the side. "I think someone is waiting for you."

Sheila glanced across the parking lot. It was Zeke. He was standing beside her car and holding a bouquet of flowers in his hand. At that moment she was so glad to see him. Her heart filled with so much love. He had come back to her, with her problems and all. He had come back.

As fast as her legs could carry her, she raced across the parking lot to him and he caught her in his arms and kissed her hard. And she knew at that moment he was also her sunshine and that her heart would always shine bright for him.

* * *

God, he'd missed her, Zeke thought as he continued to deepen the kiss. Two weeks had been too long. And the more she flattened her body to his, the more he wanted to take her then and there. But he knew some things came first. He pulled back to tell her how much he loved her. But before he could, she began talking, nearly nonstop.

"I'm sorry, Zeke. I should have been more supportive of you like I wanted you to be supportive of me. And you were right, I do have a problem, but I promise to work on it and—"

He leaned down and kissed her again to shut her up. When he pulled his mouth away, this time he handed her the flowers. "These are for you."

She looked at them when he placed them in her hands and for a moment he thought she was going to start crying. When she glanced up at him, he saw tears sparkling in her eyes. "You brought me more flowers after how mean I was to you on the phone?"

"I know you were upset, but your being upset was not going to keep me away, Sheila."

She swiped at a tear. "I'm glad you think that way. I thought your plane had gotten delayed. How did you get here so fast?"

"I called my dad and asked a favor. I needed to get here for you, so I swallowed my pride and asked my father if I could borrow his jet and its crew to get me here ASAP."

He knew the moment the magnitude of what he'd said registered within Sheila's brain. The man who had never asked his father for anything had asked him for a favor because of her.

"Oh, Zeke. I love you so much," she said as fresh tears appeared in her eyes.

He held her gaze. "Do you love me enough to wear my last name, have my babies and spend the rest of your life with me?"

She nodded as she swiped at her tears. "Yes."

It was then and there, in the parking lot of the TCC, he dropped down on his knee and proposed. "In that case, Sheila Hopkins, will you marry me?"

"Yes. Yes!"

"Good." He then slid a beautiful ring on her finger.

Sheila's mouth almost dropped. It was such a gorgeous ring. She stared at it and then at him. "But... how?"

He chuckled. "Another favor of my dad. He had his personal jeweler bring samples on the plane he sent for me."

Sheila blinked. "You father did all that?"

"Yep. The plane, the jeweler and a travel agent on board."

She lifted a brow. "A travel agent?"

Zeke smiled as he stood and reached into his pocket and pulled out an envelope. "Yes, I have plane tickets inside. We'll marry within a week and then take off for a two-week honeymoon in Aspen over the Thanksgiving holidays. I refuse to spend another holiday single. Since neither of us knows how to ski, Aspen will be great— we'll want to spend more time inside our cabin instead of out of it. I think it's time we start working on that baby we both want."

Sheila's heart began to swell with even more love. He'd said she was his temptation, but for her, he would always be her hero. Her joy.

"Come on," he said, tucking her hand firmly in his. "Let's go home and plan our wedding...among other things. And before you ask, we're taking my car. We'll come back for yours later."

Clutching her flowers in her other hand, she walked beside him as she smiled at him. "You think of everything."

He chuckled as he tightened her hand in his. "For you I will always try, sweetheart."

And as he led her toward his car, she knew within her heart that he would. He was living proof that dreams did come true.

Epilogue

Just as Zeke had wanted, they had gotten married in a week. With Summer's help she was able to pull it off and had used the TCC's clubhouse. It was a small wedding with just family and friends. Brad had been Zeke's best man and Summer had been her maid of honor. And her new friend, Abigail Langley, had helped her pick out her dress. It was a beautiful above-the-knee eggshell-colored lace dress. And from the way Zeke had looked at her when she'd walked down the aisle, she could tell he had liked how she looked in it.

As nothing in Royal could ever be kept quiet, there had been mention of the wedding and small reception to be held at the TCC in the local papers. The story had been picked up by the national news wires as a follow-up to the stories about Zeke's heroics in the Miguel Rivera arrest.

Apparently, news of the wedding had reached as far as Houston and Atlanta.

Cassie had arrived with her short Texan in tow, and Sheila could tell she was trying real hard to hook him in as husband number six. Even Lois had surprised her by showing up with her family. It seemed Ted intended to take advantage of the fact Zeke was now his brother-in-law.

Then there were the Traverses. Lois's mouth dropped when she found out Zeke was one of "those" Travers. But she was smart enough not to ask Sheila for any favors. Sunnie was there dressed in a pretty, pink ruffled dress and it was quite obvious that Brad was quite taken with his niece. Sheila was Sunnie's godmother and Zeke was her godfather.

"I can't get over how much you and your siblings look alike," she whispered to Zeke, glancing around. "And your father is a handsome man, as well."

Zeke threw his head back and laughed. "I'll make sure to tell him you think so."

He glanced across the room and saw Brad talking to Abigail. They sure seem a lot friendlier these days, and he wondered if the truce would last when the election for president of the TCC started back up again. But for now they seemed seen to have forgotten they were opponents.

He glanced back at his wife, knowing he was a very lucky man. And they had decided to start working on a family right away. And he was looking forward to making it happen. "We'll be leaving in a little while. You ready?"

"Yes." Sheila smiled as she glanced over at Sunnie, who was getting a lot of attention from everyone. She appreciated the time she had spent with the baby.

"What are you smiling about?" Zeke leaned down to ask her.

Sheila glanced back at her husband. "You, this whole day, our honeymoon, the rest of our lives together…the list is endless, need I go on?"

Zeke shook his head. "No need. I know how you feel because I feel the same way."

And he meant it. She was everything he'd ever wanted in a woman. She would be his lover, his best friend and his confidante. The woman who was and always would be his temptation was now his wife. And he would love and cherish her forever.

* * * * *

PASSION

For a spicier, decidedly hotter read—
this is your destination for romance!

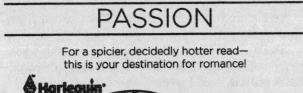

Harlequin *Desire*

COMING NEXT MONTH
AVAILABLE DECEMBER 6, 2011

#2125 THE TEMPORARY MRS. KING
Kings of California
Maureen Child

#2126 IN BED WITH THE OPPOSITION
Texas Cattleman's Club: The Showdown
Kathie DeNosky

#2127 THE COWBOY'S PRIDE
Billionaires and Babies
Charlene Sands

#2128 LESSONS IN SEDUCTION
Sandra Hyatt

#2129 AN INNOCENT IN PARADISE
Kate Carlisle

#2130 A MAN OF HIS WORD
Sarah M. Anderson

You can find more information on upcoming Harlequin® titles,
free excerpts and more at www.HarlequinInsideRomance.com.

HDCNM1111

*Lucy Flemming and Ross Mitchell shared a magical,
sexy Christmas weekend together six years ago.
This Christmas, history may repeat itself when they find
themselves stranded in a major snowstorm…
and alone at last.*

*Read on for a sneak peek from
IT HAPPENED ONE CHRISTMAS
by Leslie Kelly.*

Available December 2011, only from Harlequin® Blaze™.

EYEING THE GRAY, THICK SKY through the expansive wall of windows, Lucy began to pack up her photography gear. The Christmas party was winding down, only a dozen or so people remaining on this floor, which had been transformed from cubicles and meeting rooms to a holiday funland. She smiled at those nearest to her, then, seeing the glances at her silly elf hat, she reached up to tug it off her head.

Before she could do it, however, she heard a voice. A deep, male voice—smooth and sexy, and so not Santa's.

"I appreciate you filling in on such short notice. I've heard you do a terrific job."

Lucy didn't turn around, letting her brain process what she was hearing. Her whole body had stiffened, the hairs on the back of her neck standing up, her skin tightening into tiny goose bumps. Because that voice sounded so familiar. *Impossibly* familiar.

It can't be.

"It sounds like the kids had a great time."

Unable to stop herself, Lucy began to turn around, wondering if her ears—and all her other senses—were deceiving her. After all, six years was a long time, the mind could play tricks. What were the odds that she'd bump into *him*, here? And today of all days. December 23.

Six years exactly. Was that really possible?

One look—and the accompanying frantic thudding of her heart—and she knew her ears and brain were working just fine. Because it was *him*.

"Oh, my God," he whispered, shocked, frozen, staring as thoroughly as she was. "Lucy?"

She nodded slowly, not taking her eyes off him, wondering why the years had made him even more attractive than ever. It didn't seem fair. Not when she'd spent the past six years thinking he must have started losing that thick, golden-brown hair, or added a spare tire to that trim, muscular form.

No.

The man was gorgeous. Truly, without-a-doubt, mouth-wateringly handsome, every bit as hot as he'd been the first time she'd laid eyes on him. She'd been twenty-two, he one year older.

They'd shared an amazing holiday season.

And had never seen one another again.

Until now.

Find out what happens in
IT HAPPENED ONE CHRISTMAS
by Leslie Kelly.
Available December 2011, only from Harlequin® Blaze™

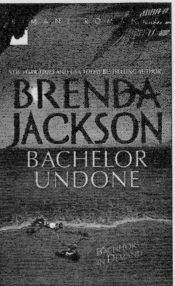

Harlequin®

nocturne™